170

Aphrodite's Blessings

Love Stories from the Greek Myths

CLEMENCE MCLAREN

Atheneum Books for Young Readers
New York London Toronto Sydney Singapore

To my editor Marcia Marshall,
for believing that I could become a writer.
To my father Edward Dobson,
who taught me to love words.
And to the girls of Anghistri,
dancing at the edge of puberty (1979–1982).

Atheneum Books for Young Readers
An imprint of Simon & Schuster Children's Publishing Division
1230 Avenue of the Americas
New York, New York 10020

Book design by Sonia Chaghatzbanian
The text of this book is set in Italian Old Style.
Printed in the United States of America
First edition
10 9 8 7 6 5 4 3 2 1

Library of Congress Cataloging-in-Publication Data
McLaren, Clemence.
Aphrodite's blessings : love stories from the Greek myths / Clemence McLaren.
p.   cm.
Contents: Running from love, Atalanta's story—Dreams of a golden hero,
Andromeda's story—For the love of a god, Psyche's story.
Summary: Atalanta, Andromeda, and Psyche, three female characters in Greek
mythology, tell the stories of their marriages. Includes information on love and
marriage in ancient Greece.
ISBN 0-689-84377-1
1. Children's stories, American. [1. Mythology, Greek—Fiction.
2. Marriage—Fiction. 3. Love—Fiction. 4. Short stories.] I. Title.
PZ7.M2235 Ap 2002
[Fic]—dc21   2001022490

Aphrodite's Blessings

*T*he Greeks called her Aphrodite, goddess of love and beauty. She sent her son Eros to shoot men and women with invisible arrows, spreading the sweet poison of love throughout their veins. The Romans changed her name to Venus and called her son Cupid—the same Cupid you see today on Valentine cards with his bow and arrows. But long before these ancient stories, before people recorded stories in writing, she was worshiped as the Mother Goddess, who brought forth each new generation to walk on this earth.

We have always adored and feared her. Even the gods were afraid of her power to make them behave like fools. The myths in this book tell of three young women who are touched by this power. One, a girl named Psyche, is willing to lay down her life to appease the goddess. Another, Andromeda, prays to escape her father's choice of husband so she can marry her own true love. A third, Atalanta, is determined to run away from love. But in the end she is transformed by Aphrodite's magic, just as we in the twenty-first century—with all our science and rationality—are transformed by love today.

RUNNING FROM LOVE
Atalanta's Story

CHAPTER ONE

A marriage offer started the series of death races that have made me famous. I always tried to talk them out of running against me. "Be reasonable," I would say. "What you have to gain is not worth losing your life." But they were so sure they could outrun me, a mere girl. And after that first foolish challenge, no one could have stopped the athletes from coming to compete, as word spread throughout Greece of the ultimate running contest —with a kingdom for a prize and death to the loser.

My father was too shrewd to turn away the young men willing to risk everything, or the thousands who came to see them race. On challenge days there were dancing bears, poets creating ballads, traders from the Orient with spices and precious stones. I would be watching from a high window in the women's quarters, fighting down the nausea. But I'm getting ahead of my story. I want to set the record straight. I'll begin at the beginning.

My mother died giving birth to me. I was the only child of Iasius, king of Arcadia. Naturally, my father wanted a son, and against the advice of his ministers, he made a substitute of me. I wore the short tunic of the athlete in training. I learned to throw the javelin and the discus, to hunt wild boar in the mountains, and when I was small, to wrestle in the courtyard with the sons of the noblemen, my body glistening with scented oil.

Above all, I learned to run. My best memories are of rising on a pink winter dawn and setting out across rolling hills, the silver leaves of the olive trees glistening in the thin sunshine. Blood pumped through my veins, warming me as I settled into my stride, and there was no sound but the thump of my feet against the earth. Alone in the hills, with the backdrop of mountain and distant sea, I raced with nature, with the wind and trees and yesterday's moon. I felt as if I could run forever.

I was rarely allowed to enjoy this solitary escape. Most mornings I reported at dawn for training at the gymnasium. No one dared oppose the king's wish to turn me into an athlete, but my coaches offered encouragement with their mouths while disapproval shone from their eyes. I wonder why my father never saw it.

The runners I trained with didn't miss a chance to trip me at the starting line, or make jokes about my girl's body. True, I could have reported their insults, but I never did. Underneath, I knew I didn't belong there, sharing their pastimes. So I hid my anger and shame and dreamed of that day when, if I worked hard enough, I might become part of their world. After all, I had much more in common with the young athletes than with girls my age, who sat in the shade with their embroidery, gossiping and giggling over marriage offers. And sometimes gossiping and giggling over me.

My cousin Filomena and her friends considered me a freak of nature. I knew this because I overheard them one day in the women's courtyard. They were curling their hair into ringlets, a tiresome procedure that took all afternoon.

"She's tall as a boy," one of them whispered, "and brown as a peasant."

"And her hair ..." My cousin Filomena saw me then and cupped her hand over her mouth.

I walked past them with long strides. Let them laugh, I told myself. I had better things to do than twist rags into my hair. I usually brushed it away from my face and tied it with a ribbon at the base of my neck, but when I raced, it often worked free and streamed out behind me.

Both hair curling and embroidery had to do with pleasing a husband. Here, too, I had nothing in common with my cousin and her friends, even though I was fifteen, of marriage age, just as they were: Fifteen was not too young to produce sons. And how silly they were about the mating ritual—the sidelong glances exchanged in the courtyard, the whispered messages behind stone columns—while upstairs in the palace fathers argued over dowry.

Aunt Marusha, my father's sister, had recently taken up the chore of getting me married.

"You're never going to get a husband if you don't learn to weave and embroider," she would remind me. "And stop running around in that disgraceful tunic."

I enjoyed arguing with her. "That's not so," I would say. "We both know I'm a prize in the marriage market, even if I never embroider a stitch."

This truth gave me no joy, and, more and more, I found myself worrying about my own excellent prospects. On the day following this particular argument, I brought up the problem with my tutor, Nestor, in the middle of a philosophy lesson.

"None of them would want me if it weren't for the kingdom they'll inherit by marrying me," I told him.

"Well, well, well," Nestor said, setting down the scroll he'd been reading. "Is that what's distracting you. This marriage business?"

Nestor was an elderly Athenian who taught me mathematics and philosophy after my training at the gymnasium. He was short and round, with a fringe of white hair and eyes that were always sad, even when he smiled. He was also my friend, the only person who ever really talked to me.

"My cousin makes jokes about my muscles," I said, stretching my long, tan legs. "My aunt says no man would want a girl with legs like these. Not that you can ever see their legs," I added with a laugh, thinking of the trailing robes worn by our women, the kind my aunt Marusha wanted me to wear.

Nestor sat looking at me for a long time. It was

that heavy hour of late afternoon that's no good for anything but dreaming, and I was used to his silences. I waited, hoping he would find words for my fears.

"You don't know how beautiful you are," he finally said. "No one has allowed you to see yourself. Your tall, graceful form, your dark hair flying behind you as you run ..." He paused, pinching his chin. "I think perhaps they're scared to death of you, all those would-be suitors. You challenge their reality."

The word "reality" reminded Nestor of our abandoned philosophy lesson—we'd been talking about whether one can ever know what is real—and I was left to ponder his remarks in silence. Me beautiful? And what did he mean about challenging their reality? Like most philosophers, Nestor was better at asking questions than at answering them. And in the end he was wrong about one thing. The men in our kingdom were not scared to death of me. But they should have been.

I, too, should have seen what was coming. I should have noticed how, increasingly, Aunt Marusha would nag my father about what I'd become with his encouragement.

"Just because Zeus has not given you a son, you have no right to turn Atalanta into a substitute," she would say, pursing her thin lips into a network of wrinkles. "It's not natural for a girl to be an athlete. To run around half naked. People are talking."

He laughed at her lectures. "My daughter is a better athlete than most of the sons in this kingdom. They're all jealous!"

My father had been a champion runner in his youth. Since he'd become a spectator, he was even more obsessed with sporting contests. In our state, athletes were honored above all others. So in spite of my aunt's resistance, my father seemed content to monitor my progress as a runner. And I foolishly believed it might be enough for him if I could become the best in our kingdom.

A month before I turned sixteen, I ran my two best times. My father was thrilled with my progress. When he summoned me on the morning of my birthday, I thought he wanted to discuss the coming regional games, and that he might finally allow me to attend. I was smiling as I approached his throne. Father was a handsome man, tall, with hair turning silver at the temples, and a full beard he was quite vain about. I remember thinking he looked exactly the way a king is supposed to look.

I didn't know that his advisers, who were seated around him, were calling me a disgrace to the kingdom. Rather than see a woman rule, they were threatening to put a cousin on the throne after his death.

"We have to talk about marriage," he told me, glancing at his nobles. "They fear a civil war if I die without a male heir."

I hung my head, searching for arguments. "What about the games next month?"

"There will be no more games." He nodded at me and cleared his throat. "It's time, Atalanta."

Excuses raced through my head. Could I remind him of the oracle who had prophesied that marriage would be the end of me? No, my father assured me that such predictions could be averted, with sacrifices to the right gods. But the oracle's words had terrified me—still terrified me.

I took a deep breath, just as I had learned to do to ease my panic before a race. I turned to the ministers, who were watching with satisfaction. I wanted to shout at them, "How can I become the bride of one of the nobles who mocks me every day at the gymnasium? How could I no longer be allowed to run!"

"I can't," I whispered.

Father was frowning, impatient. "We've had offers from all the best families, so many that my advisers are concerned about dissension within the kingdom. We have to find some way of selecting one without offending the others." He sighed heavily.

"Ah, Atalanta, would that we could go back to the days when our biggest problem was to take two seconds off your starting time."

"I can't," I said, louder this time.

"Come now, you act as if we're talking of selling you into slavery."

I looked up, eyes wide. That was exactly what we were talking about. And I realized with a shock that he was never going to understand. He was a man.

CHAPTER TWO

As I dashed through the courtyard to share the awful news with Nestor, a voice called my name. I recognized the tone of mockery before I saw the face. It was Leonides, a talented athlete who'd brought home more prizes to our kingdom than any other. He had an angular face and curly reddish hair, and although I was almost as tall, he seemed always to be looking down at me.

I had never been allowed to travel to regional games, but I had begun to offer serious competition here at home, and Leonides didn't like it. Just the week before, I had come in second to his first in a middle-distance event. He claimed I'd jumped the line before the starter's arm fell and stalked off the field in protest. Even my second place was an affront to him.

"Have you decided which one of us will be honored with your hand—and your kingdom?" he demanded. In Arcadia, news traveled faster than the fastest runner.

"My father is seeking a way to decide among the suitors," I said, pushing past him.

"Why not a race? Give yourself to the man who can outrun you?" He grabbed my arm. "That should appeal to you. It's the only thing that appeals to you!"

I pounded on his hand with my fist, but he held fast. "You think you can outrun your destiny," he said, grinning. "But in the end you'll become someone's bride." He threw back his head and laughed. "We'll see how well your training has prepared you for that!"

After he'd gone, I stood very still, listening to his laughter echo down the corridor that leads to the athletic fields. I wanted to run after him, screaming curses. But he would have found that amusing, and I would give him no more cause to laugh at me.

"It is to be decided by a race," my father announced at the public audience that same afternoon. "What perfect fairness! And since we have

Leonides to thank for this idea, he will be the first challenger. Atalanta and my kingdom will be his *if . . .*" My father scanned the ring of expectant faces, drawing out the suspense. "If he can outrun her in four lengths of the large track."

My father's gaze rested on me, standing beside Nestor. "We shall allow one month for the two runners to prepare for this event."

The ministers looked as if they didn't know whether to welcome the solution or protest its irregularity. But one person was clearly delighted.

I stared down at the marble floor to avoid meeting Leonides's eyes. He had positioned himself so that he was grinning at me from across the hall.

Within a week of my father's announcement, the kingdom had shifted into a holiday mood. There were cockfights and chariot races with frenzied betting, morning rumors that proved false before noon, vendors selling love potions and anti-love potions in the marketplace. No one doubted that Leonides would win the race. Still, there was great excitement in the air. The problem of succession was about to be solved. Dozens of servants were working on my wedding garments, while court astrologers cast our horoscopes, arguing endlessly over signs of our linked destinies.

My father had always allowed me to wear the athlete's short tunic. Now he wanted Aunt Marusha to teach me to walk without tripping in the long robes worn by our women. She was also supposed to provide catch-up embroidery lessons.

The poor woman looked more virtuously ill-used than ever, as she hung over my shoulder observing my first botched efforts at stitching. "It's a bit late for learning to behave like other well-bred girls," she reminded me. "Po-po-po-po, too big . . . Filomena's tiny stitches are the envy of the kingdom. . . ."

"Filomena is a model of feminine virtue," I said between clenched teeth. I eased away from my aunt, who smelled of oregano and onions. "She's had ten years to perfect her tiny stitches, because she does nothing but embroider and eat. Give me more room." I plunged the needle into the wobbling cloth and stabbed my finger; blood stained the white linen.

"Po-po-po," said my aunt.

"Filomena has fat knees. She couldn't run the length of the short track if her life depended on it."

"Knees are not to be spoken of," my aunt said, pursing her lips.

"What's wrong with knees? Tell me so I can learn."

"We do not speak of knees."

"They're part of our bodies! Even if we keep them covered, we have two—one on each leg. Can we speak of legs?"

My aunt was wearing her favorite expression of pained endurance. "Legs are not to be spoken of."

"Our men believe the human body is as important as the mind and soul. Should we not feel the same?"

"It's a blessing that the gods have spared your mother from having to hear such talk," she intoned, eyes cast upward.

I should have known better than try to engage Aunt Marusha in logical discourse. Like most women, she had no use for logic. Instead, she had a series of firm beliefs, which she clung to against all reason.

"Knees, knees, knees!" I shouted out the window. I slammed my embroidery hoop on the table and ran out of the room.

I wanted to find my cousin Filomena and grab a handful of her carefully curled bangs. I wanted to hang her embroidery hoop around her neck. But I dealt with my anger the only way I knew. I wrestled out of my long robe and put on my old tunic. Then I left the palace to run in the hills.

But the next morning I had to endure another lesson. My stitches were no better, my aunt as long-suffering as ever. This time I was able to escape to Nestor's library.

"Look at this." I laughed and thrust the embroidery into his hands. "Have you ever seen such a mess?"

Nestor did not share my laughter. "It's like throwing the javelin or getting off to a clean start in a race," he said. "A skill to be mastered." He looked down at the tangled threads and sighed. "Some will be better than others, but with practice, anyone can make a fair showing."

"I don't want a fair showing!" I began to feel afraid; Nestor was supposed to be my friend. I kicked the train of my new robe. "I have no time to be learning new skills, or wearing ridiculous garments that don't allow me to move. I'm supposed to be training!"

"Atalanta, sit down here beside me. Think for a moment of your father's predicament."

I remained standing, refusing to meet his eyes.

He sighed again. "I think your father regrets having raised you with certain . . . unrealistic expectations." He was silent a moment, then, drawing in his breath, he said, "The freedom you've enjoyed cannot go on forever; the sooner you accept that reality. . . . Come, now. Sit down."

"I don't want to sit down. And I don't want to talk about reality." But my legs had gone limp; I lowered myself into a chair.

Nestor patted my hand and went on. "Athletic contests were developed to keep our men fit for war during times of peace. Running, throwing, wrestling, each had a specific purpose. Our women learned other skills, no less vital to the state. . . ." He glanced at me then, and shook his head sadly. "Forgive me, Atalanta, always I am the philosopher before I am the man."

He handed me the hoop. "The truth is this: The

month's training is for *you*. To learn how to behave as a woman. Leonides doesn't need to train." Before I could protest, he asked, "Have you ever once out-run him?"

"Once, almost."

"Almost will make you a bride. That's the reality you must accept."

I stood, still clutching the foolish hoop in front of me, then left the library without a word. Though the afternoon heat hung heavy over the valley, I felt suddenly cold. I went and sat on top of the palace walls, looking down at the deserted track.

Could Nestor be right about the month's training? I had not seen Leonides training. He and his friends had been celebrating, with more than the usual wine and bawdy jokes—most of them, I imagined, at my expense. Were they laughing at my poor attempts to enter the world of women?

I didn't want to think about the answer to that question. I changed clothes and left the palace. I ran in the opposite direction from town, passing small farms on my way to the mountains. Locusts shrilled their summer song in the olive trees, which were heavy with silvery fruit. My footsteps soon fell into their comforting rhythm.

As I climbed higher, the air became cooler. I didn't want to risk a sprained ankle, so I forced myself to slow down each time I came to a rocky section of trail. Still, I kept a rapid pace, stopping only to drink from the streams and, once, to eat a wild orange.

Just past noon, I stopped to rest on a flat rock. From my perch, I could see the entire valley, rimmed by blue-gray mountains. The miniature walls of our city shimmered in the hazy sunshine.

I looked up at the sun filtered through a canopy of mountain laurel. In the sanctuary of Delphi, oracles chewed the leaves of this plant, believing it would help them enter a dream world of hidden truth. I thought about what questions I would ask them.

Was I destined to submit to the drudgery of embroidery? To spend my life producing borders for Leonides's tunics and sons to carry back athletic prizes? Or worse, was I destined to die in child birth just as my mother had? I pressed my hands against the warm granite. Was that the meaning of the prophecy that marriage would be my ruin?

Nestor would say that only the gods know our

fate. Mortals can chew mountain laurel and utter prophecies, but we can only guess. Still, Nestor was mortal, too. Surely he believed he was helping me face the truth. But he didn't know my future any more than I did.

I sat up straight, hugging my knees. I took a long breath, considering my choices, just as Nestor had taught me to do. The truth was this: Leonides was the last man I would choose for a husband. And I was still free to try to win that race. I felt tension drain from my shoulders. I had a month to train. I would train as I had never trained before.

After awhile, I stretched out on the warm stone and drifted into laurel-scented sleep. That's when I had the dream. I call it a dream, but it was more like the plays staged by traveling actors. The torch-light fell on Leonides, who was guest of honor at a banquet, the other athletes seated around him. Their faces wore expressions of shock and something else, perhaps anger. One of them seemed to be making an effort not to cry.

Leonides was clutching a goblet with a border design of seashells and half-moons. As he lifted it to his lips, he seemed terribly sad, and that sadness caught at my heart.

I set off for the palace at a run. With the trail downhill, I arrived in little more than an hour. I don't know what I expected to find in the hall, but it was the usual early evening scene, men reclined on couches or playing draughts, mingled odors of wine and garlic, dogs fighting over thrown tidbits.

Leonides was presiding over his admirers, just as in my dream. He smiled when he saw my short tunic and dusty legs and toasted me silently with an ordinary wine cup. I lowered my eyes and left the hall. I should have felt relieved. Instead, I felt a rush of unreasonable guilt as his face, the way it had appeared in my dream, flashed in my mind's eye.

During the final weeks I was allowed to escape to the mountains every day. They all seemed to have forgotten about me in the preparations for the great race. My aunt, too busy for embroidery lessons, was shouting herself hoarse, issuing orders to servants too frazzled to listen. Nestor was writing invitations to the other Greek kings.

Seven of them announced their intention to

attend. "They're finally starting to take notice of us," my father told me, beaming with pride.

Never in my life had I enjoyed such freedom. My distance runs became longer each day. I reasoned that the uphill training would make it easier when I raced on a flat surface.

On the morning of the race, I was astonished at the number of people crowded into the field below the palace. The stadium bleachers reserved for nobles were completely full. Hundreds of other men were jostling for a better view behind barriers intended to keep them off the track.

"Fools! Have they nothing better to do?" I asked Nestor.

He shook his head, averting his eyes. I thought he was commenting on human nature, the need to be always looking for a spectacle. Clearly, I was a novelty in all the Greek lands. But something else had attracted the crowds, and at the time, I was the only one who didn't know what it was.

I watched Leonides and his retinue enter the field. Two men had skins of wine slung over their shoulders. They approached with the usual backslapping, and when they saw me, a whispered joke made them shout with laughter.

I looked closely at my opponent. There was something slack about him. His skin had lost that vital glow of the athlete in training. I felt a nameless fear as I watched him limbering up.

Then, from the royal box, my father signaled us to approach the starting line. Scanning the stadium, I saw the crowd transformed into a thousand-headed beast, screaming for blood. I reached for Nestor's hand.

"You cannot choose your destiny, my child," he said. Gently, he turned my shoulders so that I faced Leonides. "All you can do is walk toward it with dignity."

CHAPTER THREE

*T*he event called for us to race four times up and down our largest track. It ran the length of the palace walls, with stadium seating at the starting line, which was also the finish line.

I remember the smell of sunbaked dust as I crouched at the start. I remember the shouts of the crowd, the blur of the faces behind makeshift barriers that lined the field. I felt light-headed with fear. I had competed in games here at home in the past year, but never before so many spectators.

The starter raised his arm, signaling for silence. A hush fell over the crowd. I glanced at Leonides's profile—a mistake. He looked relaxed, confident. Then the starter's arm fell, and my body burst from its coiled crouch. My start was good, but my opponent's was better, and his lead increased in the first length. As I found my stride, he was already ahead, running smoothly, arms low and close, legs working easily. I had always admired the efficiency of his form.

I knew I had to stay close, to avoid losing ground. I concentrated on running as smoothly as he did. Fifteen paces ahead, he reached the turning post, slowed, and swung around it. Coming back now, his eyes mocked me as we passed.

I picked up precious seconds at the post because I was lighter and could reverse direction more quickly. I gained steadily in that second length, which led back to the starting point. The crowd roared as the gap between us narrowed. Leonides took the second turn clumsily, reversing direction and coming back toward me. Our eyes met as we passed once more. This time I saw fatigue and a spark of panic. Somehow our race had become a true contest—with the outcome in doubt. The crowd sensed it, too.

In the third length I entered a quiet place, a place with no pain, my body moving rhythmically as we raced toward the final turn. I did not hear the noise of the crowd. There was only the thump of my feet and Leonides just ahead of me. I was closing the distance; he could hear my footsteps behind him.

Then, suddenly, we were running shoulder to shoulder, our sandals pounding the earth in unison. Leonides's breath came in groans as he darted an anguished glance in my direction. Approaching the final turn, I shot ahead and rounded the post ahead of him.

Seconds into that final length, Leonides sprinted past me. I focused on the back of his sweat-soaked tunic, willing it closer as I had never willed anything in my life. I concentrated on ignoring the pain. I pushed harder. The blur of faces at the finish line came into sharp focus. They were screaming for blood, and that screaming was in my throat and lungs. I swallowed it down with each burning breath.

Each footfall brought me closer. I was an arm's length from him, then a hand's length. With something like a sob, I reached into myself for that last measure of will. I pulled ahead, by less than half a stride. Suddenly, Leonides stumbled and pitched forward onto the track, and in that same instant, momentum propelled me across the finish line.

Normally one of the trainers would rush up and support a winning runner, make sure he kept moving. No one approached me. I stood there watching them shrink from me, then, turning, saw Leonides being helped to his feet. That moment is forever fixed in my memory, the droop of his shoulders as he staggered forward, the pallor of his skin under the gloss of perspiration. Most of all, I remember the stricken look on his face. I had seen it before in my dream.

Nestor came and led me off the track. I expected to hear congratulations from him, at least. His face grim, he poured me a cup of water without comment. What was wrong? I'd won, hadn't I?

A buzz rippled through the crowd when my father came forward in the royal box. For a moment he seemed to be urgently conferring with the priests, then he lifted both arms for silence. His voice fell into the hush of a thousand gaping mouths. "You who have gathered here know the conditions of this race...."

I smiled, savoring the moment. I had won my

freedom, at least temporarily. There would be no royal wedding.

Always the showman, my father paused before continuing. I was lifting a jar of water to pour over my head when I heard him say, "Leonides's run to marriage or to death...."

I froze, forcing myself to listen, to make sense of the words.

"Leonides has chosen to be put to death by his fellow athletes...."

My jar fell to the ground and shattered, water disappearing into the parched earth. I could no longer make out what my father was saying because of the buzzing of the crowd. Or was it in my head?

"Death?" I mouthed at Nestor.

His nod was my answer.

The other athletes carried Leonides off the field on their shoulders, reverently, as if he were a hero returning with a great prize. Not one of them looked my way. I fought the urge to look at my opponent. I was afraid of the terrible sadness on his face. I stood there, rooted to the earth, taking deep breaths. The crowd was absolutely silent.

❤ ❤ ❤

I didn't have an explanation until later that day, when Nestor returned to his rooms. "Why didn't you tell me?" I said accusingly.

"What difference would it have made? You had your race to run and he had his." Nestor was quiet a moment, shaking his head. "Leonides proposed the idea of death to the loser. He insisted on it. It was his choice."

"It should have been *my choice!* I hated him, but I never wanted him to *die.*" I wiped my eyes with the back of my hand, determined to conquer the angry tears that had shaken me for the past hour. "You're the one who has tampered with destiny. I would have let him win!"

"Are you so sure of that?"

His question silenced me. Would I have let Leonides win if I had known? The truth was, I really wasn't sure.

Nestor held out a basket of bread and cheese. "You haven't eaten since last night," he said softly.

I did not reach for the food. "Leonides will never feel hungry again," I said, and the tears came again.

My enemy had been dead more than an hour.

It was early evening. The palace was plunged in unnatural stillness, no servant chatter, not even the locusts or birdsong.

"Why did he do it?" I whispered.

"Can't you guess?"

I shook my head.

"Think of his upbringing." Nestor glanced at me with his probing, teacher expression. When I didn't answer, he said, "It was a matter of pride. You knew him. How could Leonides live with the shame of being beaten by a girl?"

"I can't believe my father would have allowed it. Or the priests."

"The priests went along easily enough. Talked about auspicious signs they had read, making Leonides' stipulation agreeable to the gods." Nestor snorted with disdain. "Auspicious signs! What self-serving nonsense. Leonides's run to marriage or to death was the most spectacular thing that ever happened in our little Arcadia. Look at all the attention it's brought us."

"And my father didn't want me to present a bad showing. Or refuse to run," I said slowly. "I was the freak that seven kings came to see. He didn't want

31

to disappoint them." I turned away, biting my lip. "That's why the servants drifted apart whenever I interrupted their gossip."

"The king swore us all to silence."

I sat down and covered my face with my hands. "Immortal gods! It was my fault! Because I wanted to wear the athlete's tunic." I looked up, suddenly remembering the end of the race. "What happened to him at the finish line? Could he have miscalculated and pushed ahead too soon? Leonides knew better than that."

"Panic. Pure panic." Nestor knelt beside me and clasped my hands. "It was not your fault, nor was it his. We mortals are all living out our destinies—"

"Don't talk to me of destiny!" I pulled away and jumped to my feet. "You conspired with them to keep this from me. You're as bad as the rest of them!"

Minutes later, I burst in on my father and his council, interrupting their meeting. "How did he die?" I demanded. The ministers gave slanted looks of reproof.

"He was offered hemlock; he simply went to sleep," my father said, as if speaking of a favorite dog or horse. "Didn't Nestor explain it to you?"

"Were the other runners seated around him?"

"Of course. It was a noble end. His friends beside him—"

"The goblet he drank from, was it gold, with a border design of half-moons and seashells?" My voice sounded hollow in the marble hall.

"Yes, pure gold. A ceremonial vessel kept in our vaults. You've seen it, then?"

"I've seen it," I echoed.

"Three more suitors wish to race. We're here discussing whether you will race against them one at a time or all together."

I stared down at my shadow, distorted by the flame of the oil lamp. "I won't race against them." I swallowed, then said, "I'll marry anyone you say."

"That is not your choice," said one of the ministers, a man named Agartos, who had always been more outraged than any of the others by my boyish behavior. Now, however, he was determined to see me run. "You're a woman," he said. "You do not dictate conditions."

My father looked away. I knew I could not count on his help, no matter what I argued.

There was nothing left to say, and my rage had burned itself out, leaving me numb with exhaustion. I went outside to the courtyard, the ancient stars circling above my head, my mind spinning with questions. Up on the mountain I'd been given a preview of Leonides's death. Had the gods sent that dream as a warning of the price I would pay to retain my freedom?

I shivered, wondering what else they had in store for me—and who would be the next opponent in this terrible contest.

CHAPTER FOUR

*L*eonides had a friend named Antillon who had loved him to the point of hero worship. He became the next challenger. I learned the next morning that I would race him alone, with three more contestants waiting their turns. I made up my mind to refuse all these contests. After all, my father and his ministers could not force me to run. I went at once to find Antillon at the track and tell him my decision.

"I'll agree to marry you," I told him, "so long as we skip the race."

He was kneeling, fastening the thongs of his sandal. When he looked up, I was shocked by the hatred in his eyes.

"I never asked to race Leonides!" I cried. "It was

his idea to gamble his life! I didn't know it was going to happen." Sudden tears caught me off guard, and I struggled to control them. "Let them put another dynasty on the throne. I won't race you!"

He stood up, composed in the face of my hysteria. "You will race, Atalanta. You will race against me if I have to drag you to the track and lash you in front of the spectators"—a smile flickered across his handsome face—"most of whom would be pleased to watch."

I nodded slowly. I thought, Here is how it is going to be from now on. It was hopeless to try to explain; Antillon was beyond listening. So were my father and his ministers. We stood a moment under the noon sun, taking each other's measure as tears dried on my face. I knew enough about male pride to imagine the kind of marriage Antillon had in mind. Losing the race would be the first defeat in a lifetime of humiliation. I would train in earnest, and so would he. Antillon was a champion runner. My only advantage was that he didn't know I was as angry as he was.

Still, I tried once more to appeal to my father. He refused to discuss the conditions of the race.

The king of Arcadia had always been an imposing adult who took pleasure watching me run, giving me pointers, slapping my back. I couldn't remember a single conversation we'd had about anything besides athletics. I realized now that he had never really been interested in me, that we had always been strangers.

Things were no better in the women's quarters. I suspected my cousin Filomena had been fond of Leonides, though she was promised to a much older man. Now she shrank from me whenever I came near. Since we shared the same rooms, it was impossible to avoid her.

"His death was his responsibility! He chose to die!" I said to her one morning as she was braiding her thick brown hair. She threw down her comb and turned to run away, but I blocked the doorway. "Say something!" I shouted.

She cowered like a frightened deer. "I'm not blaming you, Atalanta. It's just so sad!"

She burst into tears, and I stepped aside to let her pass. I could not comfort her. I could not even comfort myself.

I was choking with anger. I could never seem to

run it off. Most days I spent tearing along mountain trails like a wild creature. I'd made peace with Nestor, but the sight of other human beings made me almost physically ill. By the end of the month I was lean and hard. I felt I could outrun the wind.

All plans to teach me to embroider and dress properly had been suspended. I was far more useful as the girl athlete in a man's tunic. Betting on the next race had suddenly become a major occupation, with money coming from all over Greece. Two of our nobles had become full-time bankers and scribes just keeping track of it all. In spite of my previous victory, the odds were against me. Anyone betting on me would triple his money if I won a second time.

Some had taken that risk, judging from the shouts of encouragement on the morning of the second race to marriage or to death. The crowd, all men, had doubled. Carpenters had been working sunup to sundown, erecting new bleachers, and still, spectators stood ten-deep behind barriers, craning their necks to catch a glimpse of me. I felt numb, not really part of the scene, as if I were watching myself go through the warm-up exercises from the top of the stadium.

Antillon wasted no words on greetings. His black eyes flashed me a hostile glance as he crouched in the starting position, every muscle taut. I did the same, taking deep breaths to steady my nerves.

The starter's arm fell, and we both leaped forward. I pretended I was in the mountains, running against the wind. I passed him early in the second length. Rounding the turn, I saw terror on his face.

He sprinted past me at a pace I knew he could not maintain. He should have been saving a reserve of energy for the end of the race, just as Leonides should have done. The lead changed several times, with the crowd roaring itself hoarse. Each time I passed, I could see him fading. There was a desperate quality about his stride; he had lost his rhythm.

He ran himself to exhaustion before the final turn. I won by almost a quarter of a length. This time I heard cheers for me, doubtless from bettors who had just tripled their money. Still, when they carried Antillon to his death, the crowd fell silent, again, and a thousand heads turned to follow the procession off the field.

I didn't know if anger or destiny had given me this second victory. I did not want to think about it. Throughout the race, I'd felt more like a spectator than a participant—and strong, wonderfully strong, as if I could fly through the air without touching the earth.

After Antillon, two more challengers from Arcadia gave their lives. Then they came from Sparta, Athens, and the islands, as word spread throughout Greece of what people were calling the ultimate running contest of all time. My father, delighted with our new prosperity, enlarged the stadium and built an inn and two tavernas.

The odds were in my favor now. I had become a celebrity. I couldn't leave the palace without being stopped by fans; even some brave-hearted girls brought me flowers. I was living my dream, the state's finest runner, perhaps the finest in all the Greek lands. But it gave me no joy. I felt like a monster, demanding more and more living sacrifices.

And still, I could not stop my winning.

"I always plan to let them get ahead," I told Nestor. "Then the starter's arm falls, and suddenly I'm flying through the air, the faces of the crowd whizzing by." I knelt beside his chair. "The last race, I made up my mind to lose. That young Macedonian—I'm haunted by his face. He seemed gentler than the others. I tried to talk him out of racing against me."

"And he refused to listen."

"Yes!"

"Then it was his choice; he knew the odds."

"But, *why?* Why must they keep coming? Have they so little regard for their own lives? The next one—Kiros, the Athenian—is even less likely to listen." I took a breath and let it out slowly. "Why can't I let him win and put an end to it?"

"When it comes time for you to lose your race, you shall do so."

I shook my head sadly. "The truth is, I'm afraid to lose. Remember the oracle's words . . . about my destiny?"

"I have it written down somewhere. 'A husband is not to be yours. Avoid having one, or you will cease to be.'"

"That's what marriage would be like," I said slowly. "I *would* cease to be; would become a prisoner inside my husband's house. Never allowed to leave except on festival days. Have my body burdened by a string of pregnancies."

Nestor's eyes were pools of sadness. Even he

could find no reassuring words for the powerless-
ness of a married woman.

"*If* I even survive," I said with a bitter laugh.
"My own mother died in childbirth." I twisted away,
biting my lip. "Maybe that's why I run to win. But
oh, Nestor. Surely the gods will punish me for all the
killing."

CHAPTER FIVE

Visions of heavenly vengeance filled my dreams. Aphrodite, goddess of love, was in charge of seeing that people got married and carried on the human race. She could be ruthless when crossed. How would she punish a young woman who had killed off a succession of prime suitors?

I was so immobilized by thoughts of Aphrodite's vengeance that I couldn't even train for the next race. For days I stayed in bed, gazing out at the mountains. I finally roused myself, determined to visit my favorite place one more time, perhaps my last.

Muscles sore from disuse, I kept to the back alleys to avoid the pre-race crowds in the shops and tavernas behind the stadium. Some young boys recognized me and ran alongside, but soon tired of the pace. When I reached the foothills, I breathed more easily and fell into something of my old rhythm.

Finding my favorite rock still warm from the morning sun, I stretched out on my back, arms folded behind my head. I contemplated the row of peaks rising to meet a cloudless blue sky. A conical mountain stood higher than the others, crowned with snow. I liked to think of that perfect peak as Mount Olympus, where the immortals lived, though I knew Olympus was farther north. I felt protected here, as if some god could reach down and hold me in the palm of his great hand.

For this next race the odds had shifted to my opponent, an Athenian named Kiros, who was champion runner in all the Greek lands. His credits were such that beating him seemed impossible, no matter what success I'd had with the others. I was surprised to feel relieved that this time I would not have to make a choice.

Then I tried to imagine what marriage to Kiros would be like. I wanted to think that, even married, I could escape to the mountains from time to time, to this clearing. I could not have survived the past year without its healing solitude. But I knew the truth was otherwise. Like most noble wives, I would be confined to the women's quarters, rarely permitted to leave the house, and then only in the company of my husband. Giving up running in the mountains would be like giving up life, just as the oracle had predicted. And imagining that dreadful future, I prayed the gods would allow me to win one more time.

"Please," I said out loud, testing my echo in the immense stillness. "I cannot give up my mountains."

"They're not your mountains," said a voice behind me.

I jumped to my feet, expecting to see one of the immortals come down from Olympus. Instead, a figure of human proportions stepped from behind a tree. He was tall and beautiful in the way of the people from the North, with sun-streaked hair and eyes the color of new olives.

"They don't belong to anyone. Even the gods don't claim them. I wasn't really eavesdropping," he added apologetically. "I was standing over there looking at the view. Forgive my bad manners." He bowed from the waist. "Milanion, from Thrace."

It never occurred to me to be afraid, though there were robbers who preyed on lone travelers. I suddenly thought of how terrified my cousin Filomena would be in this situation. "My name is Filomena," I told him.

I don't know why I gave my cousin's name, except that I didn't want to be identified with the princess who had caused some of Greece's finest athletes to die.

He shot me a curious glance, as if wondering what an unescorted female was doing here alone, then picked up his pouch and came to join me. "Come, Filomena, share my lunch."

I stood biting my lip as he knelt to unpack dried figs, a loaf of bread, and some cheese. His tunic was of the finest linen, fastened with a gold clasp. "Why are you traveling on foot?" I asked, sitting down beside him.

"My horses are tethered on the main trail, my men watching over them. But I'm on a voyage of discovery, so I leave the trail from time to time, to see the country and meet the people. . . ." He handed me a fig. "And look what my wandering has led me to—a mountain nyad, perched on a rock."

I felt myself blushing. "What is it you hope to discover?"

"I'm on my way to confirm a rumor, which has spread all the way to my home in Thrace." He leaned forward and peered into the valley. "In the city of Arcadia, which should be down in that plain, a young woman has offered herself and her kingdom to any man who can outrun her. If he loses the race, he's put to death. Her name is Atalanta. Perhaps you've heard of her?"

I was examining a laurel leaf in the palm of my hand. "Everyone has heard of her—and what you say isn't true." I crushed the leaf between my fingers. "She didn't offer herself. She wanted no part of it. A runner named Leonides proposed the race as a way of deciding among suitors. It was his idea that the loser be put to death."

The Thracian was quiet, studying my profile.

"Everyone around here knows that, too," I said.

"With such high stakes, why should runners continue to try for her?"

I met his clear, green eyes. It was a question I had asked myself a thousand times.

He said, "She must be very beautiful."

"Maybe they keep coming because they can't believe they'll lose to a girl."

"They should know by now that's not true."

"It may be they're pitting themselves against death. Like the bull dancers in Crete. It's a challenge they're seldom offered in peacetime."

He nodded, frowning. I had a flash of worry that he was on his way to present himself as a contestant. But his next words quieted my fears. "I think they're foolish to risk their lives over a race, or a woman. Life is too precious." Leaning back, he held his face to the sun. "In any case, I want to observe tomorrow's race. I saw Kiros run at the games in Olympia. I want to have a look at Atalanta, too. I hear there are women coming to watch."

"A few. At the last two races."

"In my country, women join men at sporting events. Apparently that custom is catching on here in Greece. Some women were at the winter games in Olympia."

"Isn't that forbidden?"

"It used to be. In the past, there were always a few who couldn't resist the temptation and sneaked in disguised as men. When they were caught, they were thrown off a cliff."

"Beasts," I whispered.

He glanced searchingly at my face. "Times change. Perhaps one day we'll see female contestants, runners and jumpers, chariot drivers competing for prizes."

The mountain silence settled around us. Somewhere a lark trilled. I found myself remembering the cruel jokes of the athletes in the gymnasium, the fear in Leonides's eyes when he saw I might win.

"I don't think that will ever happen," I said, getting to my feet. "I have to go home. Down the hill."

He looked up, shading his eyes. I wondered if he were noting the fine linen of my tunic—or its short length. I wondered what Thracian women wore in his home state. Most of all, I wondered if he would find Atalanta beautiful when he came face-to-face with her.

"Good-bye, Filomena," he said.

A strange pulse throbbed in my neck. "Good-bye," I said. I turned to dart across the clearing, then forced myself to walk.

CHAPTER SIX

Once again, I slept badly on the eve of the race. I dreamed I was competing against a field of female runners in some future games. I saw myself winning the wreath of olive branches, which was placed on my head by Milanion, the beautiful Thracian I'd met on the mountain.

His face swam in and out of my dreams, first as finish line judge, then as a runner. I was being married to Kiros, still wearing my olive wreath. Then Kiros's face dissolved into that of Milanion. I finally gave up trying to sleep and, wrapping myself in the fleece from my bed, went outside to sit under the stars. I must have dozed off in the predawn hour and was shaken awake by Aunt Marusha.

"Po-po-po-po. Sleeping in the courtyard with the slaves and the animals," she scolded half-heartedly. Lately her words had lost their sting. She'd even placed a bet on me in the last race and come to watch me run. Like others in the palace, she'd forgotten that a man had died in order for her to collect her winnings.

"Come, child, your father wishes to see you before the morning sacrifices."

I stood stiffly and stretched. We pushed past the goats and oxen marked for slaughter that were tethered outside the men's hall. Every race day began with the sacrifice of animals to the gods, whose anger we feared and whose good will we sought in all that we did.

My father was talking with another man in the entry court. I hung back to get a better look.

"Come, Atalanta, don't dawdle," Aunt Marusha said. Even when she tugged at my arm, I refused to move. I was awake, but the face from my dreams was still haunting me.

"Atalanta, come here," my father called out. "I want you to meet Prince Milanion, from Thrace."

I stepped into the sunlight, tucking a loose strand

of hair behind my ear, suddenly embarrassed by my boy's tunic. The same pulse was throbbing in my neck. "We've already met."

"Milanion has consented to serve as judge for today's race," my father said. "We shall count on his reputation for fairness." He clapped our guest on the back. "Too bad you won't be allowed to place a bet. This promises to be our most exciting contest yet. And now, if you'll excuse me, I'm off to begin the sacrifice. Arcadia has much to be thankful for."

My father and my aunt went to join the priests, and we faced each other across an awkward silence. "The seven athletes who have died were not so thankful," I said.

"A story has reached us in Thrace that your father left you on the mountain to die because you were not the son he desired. That you were raised by a she-bear and later found your way back home. I don't suppose it's true."

I shook my head slowly. My heart was thumping as if I had just finished a race.

"Your father's right to give thanks." Milanion nodded at the stadium below on the plain, the shops and tavernas, already bustling with visitors. "In addition to all this, he's got himself the finest runner in the land—and she does what she's told." He held my gaze. "Sons are not so easily managed, Atalanta, especially talented ones."

I drew a breath, considering his remark. "How often I've wished I'd been born that son."

"Then I have much to be thankful for. I happen to like your present form—very much."

I had no experience with such compliments. Blushing furiously, I mumbled some excuse and went off to join my father. I didn't see Milanion until later, down on the field.

We had drawn the largest crowd on record, more women than ever seated among the men. The cheering sounded like the roar of the sea.

Kiros acknowledged me with a curt nod and concentrated on his stretching exercises. Crouched beside him at the start, I caught his eyes, which were empty of all emotion. The night before, I had again decided to lose the race, but as I studied his angular, hairy body, I found myself wanting to win as never before.

The wait for the start seemed endless. My throat

was so tight with fear, I thought I might choke. Would the gods have given me magical speed only to lose to this sullen stranger? Could he be my destiny?

Then the starter's arm fell, and we sprang forward, leaving a cloud of dust. I ran wildly, without strategy, taking an early lead and wearing myself out too early in the course.

At the start of the third of four lengths, the shouts of the crowd told me Kiros was closing the distance. I could hear his heavy breathing behind me. Then he was running alongside. For a time I matched him stride for stride, my heart bursting in my rib cage. I rounded the final turn just behind him, my legs numb, my vision blurry—a sure sign that I had used up my reserves. Gods, give me strength, I prayed.

Milanion, the Thracian, was straight ahead, seated above the finish line. I focused on his face, and I was back in my dreams, not feeling the pain. I would pull ahead or die.

I don't know whose foot crossed the line first. All I could see were faces spinning around me as I stumbled into Nestor's arms and collapsed. I awoke in the midst of a raging dispute—Kiros's men insisting he had won, my father, purple-faced, shouting that my foot crossed the finish line first. In the midst of this chaos, Milanion came forward and declared the race a draw. As Nestor led me away, I could barely see him in the crowd of bettors who had swarmed onto the field demanding their money.

Later that afternoon I learned from Aunt Marusha that Kiros had been awarded a finely wrought golden urn, a gift from the people of Arcadia. My father, in turn, had received a pair of chariot horses from the Athenians. The bettors' money had been returned and everyone's honor salvaged.

"It was all Milanion's doing." My aunt beamed. "Such a clever gentleman."

And I received the best gift of all. No one had died because of me. "I'm going to congratulate him," I said.

"You're supposed to be resting. Have you forgotten how you fainted today on the field? Gave us such a scare, I said to Filomena—"

"Where can I find him?"

"I know better than to try to argue with the likes of you," she said, clicking her tongue. "You'll find him in Nestor's quarters, talking philosophy, no doubt. Such an intelligent gentleman, and so refined."

Studying myself in the mirror, I ran a comb through my hair.

"Put some of Filomena's alkanet juice on your cheeks. Give you some color," my aunt said, smiling indulgently, and then, "He's the eldest son, heir to the throne, already a distinguished scholar."

I refused the alkanet but lingered at the mirror, fascinated with her gossip in spite of myself.

"Turns down all the girls his father proposes. Says they have no conversation." Aunt Marusha sniffed. "Since when was a wife supposed to converse?"

When I stepped into Nestor's courtyard, the two were leaning toward one another, talking quietly. They drew apart, and Milanion stood, smiling his green-eyed smile.

"Atalanta, it's good to see you up and about," Nestor said. "Come sit beside me."

The Thracian pulled up another chair, but I refused it and sat next to Nestor on the floor. I didn't know how to sit on a chair in a ladylike manner. I also didn't know how to make conversation, and my coming had put an end to theirs.

Suddenly I felt too shy to deliver my congratulations to Milanion. "How is your new pupil doing?" I asked Nestor in an effort to fill the silence. Nestor had recently been tutoring my cousin Filomena.

"Admirably. She'll be able to read her marriage contract. And she's mastered the basic sums to manage the household accounts."

"Basic sums. Is that all?"

Nestor sighed his most philosophical sigh. "Filomena has become what she was raised to be. Just as you are the product of your own unusual upbringing."

I bristled, and he added, "The world will be a better place when we learn to accept one another's differences."

"Nestor has been telling me about your embroidery lessons," Milanion said, his eyes laughing.

We smiled at one another, and I felt the tension drain from my shoulders. We sat awhile in companionable silence, the afternoon sun warm against my back. Later, Milanion told us about his country of Thrace and the lands farther north with their rivers of ice. I don't remember all that was said, except that it felt good being together and we laughed a lot.

Milanion walked me back to the women's quarters. I introduced him to my cousin Filomena, who stood twisting a curl around her finger, obviously too thrilled for conversation. For once, I wasn't irritated with her. It wasn't her fault she didn't know what to say to this handsome stranger.

I felt a new tolerance for the whole world. I obeyed my aunt without question when she insisted I go to bed, even though the sky was still tinged with rose. I stretched out between smooth linen covers, listening to the women gossiping in the hall. Every so often, there came a peal of musical laughter.

I felt newly born and no longer the heartless Atalanta of Arcadia, who brought death to Greece's bravest athletes. No new contenders had registered to race, not a single inquiry, and the fact that I'd raced to a draw with the great Kiros would discourage new entrants. Maybe now they would leave me alone.

I looked out the window at the first evening star, caught in the branches of a shadowy fig tree, as the women's laughter lulled me to sleep.

But my moment of peace was short-lived. I awoke to news of another contest, this one the most terrible of all.

CHAPTER SEVEN

*F*ilomena was shaking me awake. I heard
Milanion's name and rolled over on my back,
smiling up at her.

"It's the Thracian. Atalanta, are you listening?
He's asked for a race! We heard about it from the
slave who sweeps the men's hall. Milanion wants to
tell you himself, so pretend you don't know. Isn't
it romantic? I knew it the moment I saw you
together...."

I jumped out of bed and threw on my tunic.

"Wait, let me comb your hair—you can't meet
him like that! Atalanta!"

He was waiting in the main courtyard, an
apologetic smile on his face.

"You can't race against me!" I cried. "You said they were foolish to risk their lives over a kingdom or a woman."

"It's true I came here to make fun of the men who competed against you. But that was before I met you." He rubbed his forehead, as if working out a problem. "At first I thought you were the spirit of the glade, but I soon realized the truth."

"Why did you let me go on pretending?"

"I didn't want to spoil it. I began to think about your predicament, the kind of choices you'd been offered. I admired your courage. After you left, I couldn't get you out of my mind." He looked down at his hands. "When I met Kiros in the men's hall, I wanted to strangle him."

"You can't ask me to let you win! I'm not even sure I can. I don't know how it happens. Once a race starts, it's as if some outside force takes over."

"I ask no favors. I expect you to run with all the speed the gods have given you."

"My father would accept no other arrangement. Even for you, the penalty to the loser is death." That word—"death"—lodged in my throat and came out as a whisper. I stood hugging my arms around my waist. When he said nothing, I tried another argument. "All the others have been trained runners. I'm a trained runner! How can you hope to compete?"

"I intend to sacrifice to the gods."

"They've all sacrificed to the gods—to Zeus for strength, to Hermes of the winged feet for speed."

"Maybe they've been sacrificing to the wrong gods."

"You'll only kill yourself," I said angrily. "Surely the gods do not approve of suicide!" But even with that fear burning inside me, I could not be sure of what I would do when the starter's arm fell.

"Don't scold me, Atalanta." He took both my hands, and we stood a moment in the pale sunshine. "I don't understand this any more than you do. I only know I've found something worth risking my life for."

Chapter Eight

*T*he next morning, I was down at the track running slowly, stretching my legs, when a voice called my name.

"Atalanta, wait!"

Milanion was back at the starting post, running to catch up with me. I watched him close the distance between us. His form was graceful but inefficient, his arms too far from his torso, his knees too high, like a sprinter. When he reached my side, he was almost too winded to speak.

"Look at you, after only one length," I said. "It's not too late to call off the race. We'll go tell my father."

"Let's not talk about the race. For this one day." He smiled down at the ground, then lifted his eyes. "I'm a visitor in your country. Give me a tour."

I shook my head, arms crossed in front of my chest.

"We could go back to the mountains. We'll take a picnic."

In the distance, blue peaks shimmered against a pale blue sky in which puffs of clouds floated like misty islands. Even here in the valley the air was scented with wild oregano. He smiled, and I felt myself weakening.

"I thought we were friends," he said.

"We are friends. That's why I'm begging you to forget about the race."

His smile faded, and I felt a pang of guilt. "Please understand. When I was a little girl, an oracle prophesied that marriage would mean the end of me."

"Perhaps the prophecy meant the end of you as a separate entity—Atalanta against the world—and the beginning of a partnership. You lose yourself when you truly love another person." He reached out and took my hand. "Atalanta, I would not imprison you in the women's quarters. Thracian women have freedom to come and go. They attend banquets and festivals with their husbands. . . . We have wonderful mountains."

I kept my face tight, afraid to listen. After all, what did I really know about this stranger who had appeared to me out of nowhere?

He let go of my hand. When I turned and ran back toward the palace, he didn't call out to me. I was afraid to turn around and look at him, afraid I would go back if I saw his sad smile.

My father was polishing his armor in the men's hall. We hadn't had a war in years, but he insisted on keeping it shining himself. None of the servants were allowed to touch it.

He glanced up, eyes narrowed. Increasingly of late, he took no joy in my presence. "I suppose this has something to do with the new challenger," he said, pressing his cloth into a groove in the bronze.

"Kiros was allowed to return home after the race; everyone seems to have accepted it. Father, please." I took a long, steadying breath. "I don't want Milanion to die because of me."

"You speak of matters you do not understand."

"I understand that seven athletes have died."

"Thousands die in battle each year."

"That doesn't excuse us!"

He sighed with exasperation. Atalanta, I ask you to consider our reputation."

"What reputation?"

"Arcadia is so powerful that our *women* can

65

outrun *their* men!" He gestured with a gleaming leg guard. "Don't you see how this glorifies us in the eyes of the enemies who would like to march into this valley and take everything we've built?"

"I can still run against them and win. The contenders don't have to forfeit their lives."

"The forfeit is what gives our race its power. Leonides would be pleased at the prosperity he's brought us."

"Maybe he would prefer to be alive."

But my father had stopped listening. He didn't hear me leave. Still polishing his armor, he was gazing out the window at the stadium, a curve of marble and granite gleaming in the afternoon sun.

CHAPTER NINE

A unt Marusha held out a basket of fruit.
"You can't run on an empty stomach," she
said. "Remember what happened last time? You collapsed right there on the track!"

"No food. I don't want to be sick in front of all
those people," I told her. I was crouched in the
window, hugging my knees and watching a river of
spectators pour into the stadium. "Can't you tell
my father I'm sick?"

"They would only reschedule the race for tomorrow, or next week. Better to get it over with."

"I can always run away."

"Not on an empty stomach." My aunt set the
basket in my lap. "Filomena, bring her some honey
water," she called out before returning to the wool
she was preparing for the loom.

Filomena brought me a cup. I sipped tentatively while my cousin leaned over me and peered down at the stadium. "He's not there yet, is he? They say he's sacrificing to Aphrodite! Isn't that romantic? An athlete sacrificing to the goddess of love!"

My stomach lurched, I set the cup on the floor.

"If I were racing against someone as handsome as Milanion," Filomena said, "I'd let him win ... by just a little." She gestured with thumb and index finger.

"You're not me! I don't spend all my time in the courtyard sighing over men."

Filomena flinched as though I had slapped her, then turned to go. I was already regretting my words when she turned back, straightening her shoulders. "Do you want to grow into a bitter old woman, all alone, reliving your triumphs on the track?" She hesitated, then, "Oh, Atalanta, is it such a terrible fate to be a woman, married to a man like Milanion?"

"It's a terrible fate if I haven't chosen it myself," I said slowly. But I wasn't as sure of that as I sounded. "I'm sorry I snapped at you," I said.

"Off with you, child," Aunt Marusha said to

Filomena. "This wool is ready to be dried on the roof. Atalanta needs to comb her hair and eat an orange. Oh, and be sure you spread out the skeins properly."

"You'd better go," I said, shaking my head. My cousin and I exchanged our first smile of mutual understanding.

"I'll be down in the stadium cheering for you," she said. But when she got to the doorway, she stopped and took a short breath. "No, I won't. Don't be mad, Atalanta. I'll be cheering for *him!*"

Filomena wasn't the only one cheering for Milanion. He'd attracted a number of fans during his brief stay in our kingdom. When he stepped onto the field, a shout went up that seemed to fill the valley.

The odds were four to one in my favor. Still many had placed their money on him. They must have felt sorry for the man. After all, he was alone, with only his servants as countrymen and no credits as a runner.

More women than ever were seated in the stands. Some had embroidered his name on banners, which they held over their heads. They all seemed to have fallen for his romantic notion of sacrificing to Aphrodite instead of one of the male gods.

"They all love you," I told him, surveying the crowd, "but Aphrodite is for lovesick girls praying for a man to save them from spinsterhood. She won't help you run."

He shrugged, smiling. "Atalanta, this may be the last time we talk on this Earth. Do not pierce my heart with unkind words."

I studied him carefully. "I wish I knew what you were up to."

"Would you reveal your race strategy to me? Come, take my hand. Let us wish each other luck."

Seeing us touch, the crowd cheered wildly and shouted encouragement. My father had difficulty quieting them so the race could begin.

"Your tunic is too bulky. You'll lose speed," I told him at the starting line. He had an odd sort of pouch strapped around his waist.

"Good luck charms," he said, patting it.

"That's not the right way to crouch. Dig in your toes and raise your hips."

"Like this?'"

"You're still too stiff."

Then the starter's arm fell. I shot ahead in the first length. A vision of Milanion being carried off the field to his death flashed in my mind's eye, slowing me down. I quickly dismissed the thought. I told myself, there's still time to decide.

I rounded the first turn and doubled back toward him. He was loping along as if he had all the time in the world to complete the four lengths. When I came close enough to see his face, he took a shiny, round object from the pouch on his waist and held it in front of him. Just as our paths were about to cross, he tossed it behind me.

I whirled around to see what he had thrown. It had fallen in the dry grass at the edge of the track, but I had time to go back and fetch it. I was almost a length ahead and, besides, I needed to know what kind of game he was playing.

It was a golden apple with a delicate stem and two perfect golden leaves, each engraved with a network of veins. I felt light-headed as I stood holding it in the palm of my hand, the crowd roaring around me.

Milanion had rounded the first turn and was coming back toward me. For a second I was disoriented, not sure of which way to run. Then he was passing me, grinning and pointing at the second turn.

I set off after him, still holding the apple, although I knew its weight would throw off my stride. My breathing was wrong, I couldn't settle into my pace, but somehow I couldn't let it go. I didn't catch him until the start of the third length.

"What kind of trick is this?" I demanded between gasps.

Instead of answering, he held out a second golden sphere and juggled it from hand to hand before rolling it back toward the turn we had just rounded.

His fans were shouting hysterically. This time, I would have to backtrack an even greater distance, but anger gave me speed. Did he think he could win by cheating? I could retrieve his apples and still outrun him.

The second apple was larger than the first and surprisingly heavy. It caught the light and flashed it back like a miniature sun. Again, I felt a tingling in my fingertips as I picked it up. And, again, I felt compelled to hold on to it. With a golden apple in each hand, I bolted for the final turn, which Milanion was fast approaching.

"Cheater!" I panted when I caught him at the start of the last length. But I was impressed in spite of myself. He had managed to wipe out my lead, twice.

His answer was a look of mock innocence. He seemed no more winded now than he had been the day before after only one practice length. Clearly, he was a better runner than he had pretended to be. He pulled out a third apple, and I ran along beside him, mesmerized by its brightness. He held it up to the sun, which cast an aura around it.

When he lobbed it into the air, I stopped short, following with my eyes. A hush fell over the crowd as it sailed in a golden arc and fell to Earth. The finish line was straight ahead, the apple off the track to the right. I raced after it, stooping to pick it up without stopping.

Now I had run out of hands. I was cramming the third apple into a fold in my tunic when I saw Milanion dashing toward the finish. He had abandoned his inefficient lope and was sprinting. And still I could not let the apple go. I took off after him, the two smaller apples in my right hand while I clutched the largest in my left.

He was a hand's length ahead, arms pump-
ing, tunic soaked with sweat. For an instant, the
earth seemed to stand still. Banners stretched taut
against the bright blue sky, and the sound from the
bleachers was like Earth-mover Poseidon crushing
villages under mountains. I stumbled through the
roaring to the finish line. At first I wasn't sure who
had won. Then I saw people running to congratulate ... him!

I caught a glimpse of Nestor, who had abandoned all dignity and was jumping up and down,
clapping his hands, the old fool. People were pulling at me, offering water and good wishes. Everyone in sight was grinning. I brushed them aside,
trying to get closer to Milanion.

But his fans had crowded down onto the field,
mostly female admirers cackling like hens as they
placed a wreath on his head. I stood watching him
while the crowd swirled around me. If he hadn't
cheated, I thought, they could be carrying him off
to his death instead of crowning him with olive
branches. He had no way of knowing whether I
would let him win or not. I wasn't even certain of
what I was going to do until after the race started.

What enormous risks he had taken—to win me! I was amazed at his single-mindedness. He reminded me of myself!

Laughter bubbled inside me. I tore at the robes of the women to get close to him.

"Wait!" I heard him say. "My bride. Let her pass."

They parted at his command, and I walked toward him, holding the apples in my cupped palms.

"Aphrodite loaned them to me," he said. "Even you could not have resisted their magic."

"Aphrodite's apples!" a woman cried out.

"From the golden tree that grows in her garden in Cythera," another one said.

"I told you the others were sacrificing to the wrong gods," Milanion said, coming forward to take the apples from my hands. "Can you forgive me?"

His smile melted something inside me, a hard knot I'd been carrying for as long as I could remember. I stood there speechless, eyes filling with tears.

Aunt Marusha, who'd come up behind me, nudged me to answer him. "Of course she forgives you," she finally said. "Take my word for it, with a good husband at the helm, Atalanta will become the most obedient bride a man could wish for—"

"If he wants obedience, he should get a dog," I interrupted, "or better yet"—I smiled up at him— "marry one of the girls his father found for him."

My aunt poked me in the ribs, hard. But Milanion threw back his head and laughed. "I'll take my chances with this one," he told her.

"You won't regret it, Lord Milanion. I'll teach her to weave and embroider."

"I can hardly wait to see the results." He grinned at me. I grinned back.

"Atalanta, your father is waiting." He held out his hand. "Will you take your chances with me?"

I slipped my hand into his. I said, "I think I would have let you win."

"Aphrodite doesn't take chances," he whispered back.

Flowers rained down on us as, hand in hand, we walked toward the royal box.

DREAMS OF A GOLDEN HERO
Andromeda's Story

CHAPTER ONE

Nothing in the world angers the gods more than human pride. We can get away with most anything else if a god or goddess likes us well enough. Everyone in our kingdom of Joppa knew it was courting disaster to go around claiming to be best in the world—everyone, it seems, but my mother, Cassiopea, the queen.

Mother never worried about divine vengeance. She boasted of the abundance of our grain, the brilliance of our sunsets, my father's skill at diplomacy. And more and more as I grew older, she boasted about herself. Smiling into her mirror, maids fluttering about her, she would declare that no queen in all the world could match her beauty. Her ladies murmured agreement—it was their job to agree with the queen—but her self-flattery made them uneasy. You could see them trying not to cringe.

Mother was indeed beautiful, with pale skin and delicate features, as if her face had been fashioned out of ivory by a master craftsman. Visitors to our court called her the world's most beautiful woman—and she loved it. She seemed to thrive on this attention, like a small child. Over time, I took on more and more of her duties. I learned to stay in the background, even as I directed servants and supervised inventories. I somehow knew I had to look out for her instead of the other way around.

What I didn't know was that one day I would have to pay the price for her recklessness.

It happened soon after my sixteenth birthday. My mother sent for me. I found her in her rooms, seated in her gilded chair. One of her maids was brushing her long black hair.

"How lustrous your hair is, Queen Cassiopea," the maid was saying.

"Not a strand of gray," Mother said, then noticed me standing in the doorway. "Is there another woman who has held on to her beauty as long as I have, with a daughter ready for marriage? It's as if I were one of the immortals."

"Mother, you know it's dangerous to compare yourself with the gods!"

The queen took pride in her impulses. She liked to say the first thing that came into her mind without being reminded of the consequences. "Please, Andromeda," she said, "let's not worry about the gods. I'm sure they have better things to do than eavesdrop on me." She nodded at her reflection and waved away the maid. "Come, child, let's see a smile. As usual, you're much too somber, and this is a joyful day. We've had an offer for you. Your father is even now finalizing the details."

Her three ladies turned to watch my reaction.

"Is it Fineus?" I asked. *Please, not Fineus,* I prayed to all the gods.

The possibilities flashed through my mind as Mother and her ladies smiled playfully at one another. Two unmarried nobles, both closer to my age, had been casting looks in my direction. But Fineus, king of Tyre and a cousin to my father, had more to offer, and I knew he'd arrived at our palace the night before. I swallowed down a lump in my throat. I had learned early on to hide what I was feeling, to appear composed when I wanted to scream and stomp my feet.

"Come now, Andromeda, who else would it be?" Mother said, laughing. "He's been yearning for you ever since his wife died in childbirth. When was that?" she asked her ladies. "Six, seven years the poor man has been waiting for our Andromeda to grow up?"

I kept my face blank. I didn't want them to see my foolish disappointment. I always knew a husband would be chosen for me by my father for political reasons. Our northern territories shared a common border with Fineus's kingdom of Tyre. It was reasonable to want to unite the two states by marriage.

Why, then, was I feeling so defeated? Like all royal daughters, I was born into my destiny—subject to my father and then my husband, and when he was dead, to my sons. I had no right to wish for anything more. And yet, I dreamed of a young hero who would whisk me away from this humdrum life. I closed my eyes and conjured up his image—an athlete's body, golden hair, eyes sparkling with humor, a man who could also laugh at himself.

My mother was eyeing me suspiciously. "Whatever is the matter with you, Andromeda? Don't tell me this comes as a surprise."

"No." I looked down at the floor. "Fineus is the logical choice."

"Logical! How like my sensible daughter to use such a word to speak of her bridegroom." She got up from her chair. "Come, we'd better do something with her hair. I expect the men will be paying us a call with the happy news. Fetch the green robe with gold threads," she called to a maid.

I hated the green robe, hated the scratchy embroidery. I preferred a draped tunic without adornment. But I sat obediently as a servant twisted my hair into a braid on top of my head. Did Mother really expect me to be happy with Fineus? True, young brides were supposed to learn to love their assigned husbands. My mother seemed genuinely fond of my father, though he had little time for her. Still, I knew this fondness was not that overwhelming passion our poets called love.

I glanced at the ladies' faces, wondering what they were thinking behind their smiles. It was an unspoken law of the women's quarters that they almost never revealed what they were thinking. I wanted to shout at them, "How can you expect me to fall in love with Fineus—or even become fond of such a man?"

I pictured his small frame, his curly grayish hair, thinning at the top, the way he strutted into a room, when he had less to strut about than almost any man I knew. I pressed my fist against my lips to hold back the tears as my anger turned inward. How foolish I'd been to retreat into dreams of a beautiful young hero. I should have known this day was coming. I should have prepared myself for Fineus.

One of the maids was saying something about the highlights in my hair.

"The sea green is a perfect choice," another remarked. "It matches her eyes. Your Majesty, your daughter has inherited your beauty. Except for her lighter hair, she's a replica of you."

Mother was frowning down at me with an expression I couldn't name. "Yes, isn't it strange," she said, twisting her ivory bracelet, "we're so alike physically and so different in every other way. Andromeda, must you look so sad? We're making you a queen!"

Then the men arrived, my father, King Cepheus, followed by a train of nobles, and my future husband, who was beaming and strutting more offensively than ever.

"My dearest Andromeda . . ." Fineus took my hands. I drew away instinctively, a reaction I think he interpreted as shyness. "You are even lovelier than before, if that's possible. And *taller!*"

In the months since his last visit, I had grown as tall as he was. I could see him sizing up this new development. A husband, even an unworthy one, was to be obeyed in all things. Fineus would not want to have to look up at a wife. Would he forbid me to grow taller?

Father was explaining the details of the marriage settlement. There was my dowry, as well as trade concessions, and on the groom's side, permission for our flocks to use Tyre's greener pastures during the dry months. Finally, there was an agreement that our two kingdoms would be joined and ruled by our heirs.

Our heirs. All at once, it occurred to me that I would have to bear Fineus's children—when I could hardly stand to have him touch me. I would be judged by my ability to produce sons. I knew how that was done from listening to the gossip in the women's quarters. My eyes filled with tears.

To Mother's credit, she noticed my distress. "If you men will excuse us, I think the bride has had enough excitement for one morning," she said. "You'll see her later at the banquet."

Fineus patted my hand as if he already owned it. My father kissed my cheek. He was glowing, as always, after a successful bout of bargaining. "Such a fortunate day for both our nations," he said.

At last I was allowed to go back to my room, where my servant, Sophia, was waiting for me. "So, it's to be Fineus?" she said.

"Who else would it be?" I said angrily, struggling to remove the green robe.

Sophia stood a moment, small and dark, shaking her head, then helped me slip the robe over my head.

"I'm sorry, it's not your fault," I murmured.

She had been taken from her southern tribe in a border war and had grown up at my side. Much more than a servant, she was my best friend, my only friend. If anyone in Joppa could understand what I was feeling, it was Sophia. I suddenly realized that we were both destined to be slaves—Sophia to my family, and me to my future husband.

I sat down at the edge of the bed. "How silly of me. I was hoping for something better." Then, looking up, I said, "Mother and her ladies have no romantic notions about marriage. They think I should be happy to be Fineus's queen."

Sophia sat beside me, the dress folded in her lap.

"What's the matter with me?" I asked after awhile.

"You've already given your heart away to a golden hero who flies through the air and slays monsters. How could Fineus compete with the man who killed Medusa?"

Sophia knew of my dream lover, though neither of us had ever seen him. His name was Perseus, and rumors of him were everywhere. He'd been fathered by the great Zeus, king of the gods, or so people said. Recently he had killed a monster called Medusa. Instead of hair, her head was covered with writhing snakes, and she could turn anyone who glanced at her to stone. Until Perseus, no human had ever looked at her and lived to tell about it.

"Of course Perseus had help from the gods," Sophia reminded me.

This was true. The goddess Athena had given him her bronze shield, which he used as a mirror to see the monster's reflection instead of her face. The gods also gave him a sword, a magic helmet that made its wearer invisible, and a pair of winged sandals. Still, managing to kill Medusa without actually looking at her was an extraordinary feat, and everyone was talking about it.

To celebrate his victory, the young hero was even now flying with his borrowed sandals in search of other adventures. Peasants talked of having seen a sudden glint of gold in our own skies, which could have been that son of Zeus Almighty, gliding above the trees with the golden wings on his ankles. Sophia and I followed the accounts and spent hours looking up, hoping to catch a glimpse of him ourselves. In the meantime, I had created an image of him that I carried in my heart.

Sophia put her arm around my shoulder. "You're almost certain to outlive old Fineus," she said. "He doesn't look very robust."

"Somehow that's not very comforting."

"It could be worse."

"How?"

"They could have given you to Thestor."

Thestor was an elderly retainer who had already outlived four wives. He had a bulbous nose and scaly patches on his bare scalp. He spent his days lounging on a couch telling anyone who would listen about the meaning of life.

I smiled in spite of myself at Sophia's determination to be cheerful. She couldn't have survived as a slave in an alien land without it, and she'd taught me her own survival wisdom: Be grateful for each day's small miracles, and never cry over those things that cannot be changed. I sometimes wondered what it would take to rob her of this optimism.

That evening at the banquet, my fiancé outlined the duties of a wife: the maintenance of endless lists, the storage of wheat (in a dry place), the storage of wine (in a cool place), the arrangement of items on storeroom shelves. It was all I could do to pretend to listen.

"I see this is bewildering to you, a frivolous girl, suddenly thrust into a position of great responsibility," he said, reaching to pat me again.

I slid my hand from under his. I didn't tell him my mother's greatest frustration was that I was not frivolous enough, that I had been supervising servants in a large, complicated household for years.

"Do not despair," he said. "My housekeeper will instruct you in these arrangements, an admirable woman who has been with me for years. She is moderate in her eating and drinking habits, completely dedicated."

I knew I would loathe her.

"Why do I find him so infuriating?" I said to Sophia when I got back to my rooms. "I've always known I would be given to a husband. That I must submit to his authority. But this one! How could my parents do this to me?"

Even Sophia could find no encouraging response.

"I'll sacrifice to Artemis," I said. "She's helped other girls who refused to marry."

"By changing them into trees or flowers. Is that what you want?"

"Yes!" I took off a sandal and threw it against the wall. "And don't tell me things could be worse, because they couldn't. I'd rather die than marry Fineus!"

"Shame on you, Andromeda. You wouldn't rather die. Life is a gift worth fighting for, every minute of every day."

"What would I have to live for, married to him?"

"Red poppies on the hills. The smiles on your children's faces. Our own secret jokes. Surely you'll take me with you to Tyre; Fineus is not a man to turn down an extra slave. And don't tempt the gods by talking of death," she said, retrieving the sandal. "Things could always get worse."

She was right. Things got worse. By the end of the week, the problem of Fineus was eclipsed by events even the oracles could not have predicted.

CHAPTER TWO

I never knew what pushed my mother to bring the god's curse upon us. Maybe with the wedding preparations, all the fuss over me, she wasn't getting enough attention. Maybe she was trying to make me laugh. My glum countenance was attracting notice, even among the men. Maybe she really did think the gods were too busy to pay attention to what we mortals say here on earth.

I was standing at the mirror in the women's hall, waiting for a seamstress to finish the hem of my wedding dress. It was pale mauve, of a fine silk imported from Colchis, and saved in a chest for this occasion. I had insisted there be no embroidery, a small rebellion.

"And the final touch." Mother stepped forward

and draped a shimmering veil around my face. "I wore it at my own wedding."

"How beautiful she looks," the ladies chorused.

"Even if she's forgotten how to smile." Mother linked arms with me, facing the mirror. "Andromeda, look at us. Aren't we gorgeous?"

"Can I take it off now?"

"Surely we are more beautiful than all the other women in Joppa."

I shrugged and turned away, but she pulled me back, smiling. "We are more beautiful than all the women on all the islands of the sea," she said.

I shook my head. It was useless to reason with her.

"We are more beautiful than all the women in all the kingdoms on earth ..."

I felt a stirring of fear. The seamstress kneeling at my feet seemed to be holding her breath. No one spoke. All eyes were fixed on the queen. She smiled at our startled faces and, throwing her arms in the air, declared, "We are more beautiful than the daughters of Poseidon, lord of the sea. More beautiful than all his nymphs who swim in all the oceans of the world!"

The ladies cringed, openly.

"Mother, please. You must not say such things!"

She made a face at me, and then we heard the roar, as if all the oceans of the world were rising up against us. The ladies clung to one another as the floor buckled under our feet. Even my fearless mother reached for my shoulder to steady herself.

"What was that?" someone whispered in the hush that followed.

"An earthquake, you fools!" But Mother was holding her fingers to her lips, as if she wanted to take back her words. Everyone knew which god produced earthquakes. It was Poseidon, lord of the sea. We called him Earthshaker, and he was very attached to his numerous daughters, a band of sea nymphs called Nereids.

"You're making me jumpy with your superstitions, all of you!" she said, looking only at me. "I'm going to my rooms!"

The damage to the palace wasn't serious: some shattered pottery, a toppled garden wall. But all of us who had been there with the queen feared there would be more to come. In the walled stillness of the women's quarters, we sat waiting.

The first accounts reached the palace by night-fall. The earthquake had buried a score of houses. A flash flood had wiped out the grain harvest in our southern province; a tidal wave swept away two coastal villages.

Mother kept to her rooms. My father, who knew nothing of her boast, called a meeting of his ministers.

"Why should the god punish all those innocent people because of something said by one foolish woman?" I said to Sophia. I had asked that same question just moments before.

"Try to get some rest," she said gently.

I stretched out on my bed to wait, for what I didn't know. I did not sleep. In the morning I joined my father and his advisers in the main hall, where they were still searching for reasons to explain our bad fortune.

"It's perfectly clear, King Cepheus," Fineus was saying in his know-it-all voice. "One of you has offended some god. I have an oracle back in Tyre who's never wrong in these matters. I'll send for him at once."

"I can think of no god or goddess we've slighted,"

my father said, rubbing his beard. "We've observed the rituals. Been faithful with our sacrifices." He glanced at his priest, who confirmed this with a nod.

Then a messenger was ushered in, a boy of eight or ten in a torn, homespun tunic. "A sea monster, King Cepheus!" he cried, his eyes large and round. The men sat forward in their chairs.

For a brief moment the child seemed impressed with himself, to be speaking before the king and all the nobles. "At dawn, just as we were hauling our boats to the water," he cried. "It rose from the sea. Like a small island, with a huge snake's head! We could see red eyes burning in the dark. We couldn't believe it was real."

The boy's story emerged in starts and stops— the monster dashing their boats to pieces, as if they were toys, then trampling houses in a nearby village, ripping victims from their beds and cramming them into its mouth. His voice became weaker and weaker until my father got down from his throne and held the child in his arms. The final details of the slaughter arrived in gasps. The boy had escaped by crawling into an empty storage jug. He could hear the dying screams of everyone else in his family. His eyes told of unspeakable horrors. At length he could find no words for them.

When there was only silence and the boy's sobbing, Father lifted his eyes to the heavens. "Tell us, deathless gods, which of you has set this curse upon us?"

The elders searched one another's faces but said nothing. Even Fineus had the sense to keep his opinions to himself.

"Speak! Who among us has angered you?" My father's shout echoed from the arched ceiling.

Knowing the terrible answer to that question, I faded back into the crowd.

"Speak!" he called again.

A trembling voice answered, "I am the guilty one."

It was my mother. She must have entered the hall while the boy was telling his story. She stepped forward, dark hair falling over her pale face. I had never before seen my mother with her hair tangled or her robe wrinkled, the same lavender robe she'd been wearing the day before.

She said, "I compared my beauty—mine and Andromeda's—to the daughters of Poseidon. I boasted that we were more beautiful than all his Nereids.... I didn't mean to offend...." She lifted her head and saw there was no sympathy in any of the faces.

My father was still clutching the child's head against his chest. I wondered if he was as angry as I was at her recklessness, her need to shock. And yet I found myself feeling desperately sorry for her at the same time.

"I will pay the price with my own life," she said.

He would not meet her eyes.

"The price, Queen Cassiopea, is for Poseidon to name," Fineus said, stepping between them. "I'm sending for my oracle," he announced with a wave of his arm, and then strutted out of the room.

CHAPTER THREE

"Why should the god be so angry at us?" I asked my father. "Surely Poseidon knows his daughters are more beautiful than any mortal woman could be."

I had to repeat my question. Father was staring at a row of olive trees, his eyes glassy. I had found him in the orchard on his favorite bench, where he always went to be alone. We had just received word that the sea monster had destroyed another village.

"It isn't fair!" I said.

He sat a long time without responding. "I used to wonder about that when I was a child," he finally said. "In the old stories, some mortal was always being punished for claiming to be better than a god or goddess."

"Like Arachne. All she did was claim to be a better weaver than Athena. The goddess changed *her* into a spider." I sighed. "Everyone must know those stories but Mother."

"I think I understand it now," he said slowly, ignoring my criticism. I wondered if he'd spoken to her after last night's confession, but was afraid to ask. He seemed so determined to avoid any mention of her.

"The immortals want us to respect the natural order," he went on. "Nothing is more important— not a few villages, not a grain harvest, not even a few hundred human lives."

He reached down and stroked the head of his prize hunting dog, Lyos, sleeping at his feet. He said, "A dog has its place in the universe; a rat and a butterfly have theirs. We mortals have our place above the animals, and the gods their place above us. No man should aspire to be greater than he is. It's a sin worth punishing."

Father seemed to be thinking out loud, trying to reassure himself as well as me. His face was stiff, showing no emotion, but I had a feeling he was struggling for control.

"The people who are dying don't deserve to be punished," I said.

For a second, the mask slipped, and he looked as if he was going to cry. "The ways of the immortals are difficult to understand...." He turned away to stare at the fields. The silvery leaves of the olive trees were perfectly still; the scent of an impending storm mingled with the odor of wild oregano.

"But it's not their fault!" I insisted. "Besides, the words have already been spoken! Mother can't take them back." When he didn't answer, I said, "Must people be gobbled up while we wait for Fineus's oracle to appear? Why can't we consult our own priests?"

"We already have."

"Haven't they given an answer?"

He turned to me, the muscles in his jaw clenched tight. "They had an answer. It was unacceptable."

"But, why? Why is it that everything from Tyre is so much better than our own?"

"Andromeda, please!" He grabbed my shoulders, holding me so tightly, it hurt. "Leave these matters for people who are wiser than yourself."

I noticed how old he looked, his cheeks creased with wrinkles, his beard more gray than black. Even his voice sounded different, less hearty.

As I sat there feeling sorry for him, he was looking at me with an expression of unmasked pity. "Don't worry, my child," he said. "Fineus's oracle will be here tonight."

It was the silence that frightened me the next morning, an eerie silence, and the way the ladies were watching me. Something was wrong, something more awful than all the events of the past days.

The Tyrian oracle had arrived. He'd been casting the bones and reading the signs. Rumors were circulating, but no one would tell me what they were. Mother kept to her room, her ladies clustered outside her door.

"What news?" I asked them. "Is it about my mother?"

They turned away, avoiding my eyes. I went and stood by the window, terrified by their stiff faces. Was Poseidon demanding a blood sacrifice? Would my mother have to pay the price for her boast?

Then toward noon, Sophia came running to find me, her black hair flying out behind her. Without a word, the ladies drew back and opened a pathway.

"I'll die for you, Andromeda!" she cried, collapsing at my feet. "They can take me in your place!"

I suddenly felt removed from my body, as if watching myself from above. My fingers numb, I reached down and touched her head. "What news is this?" I said. My voice sounded strange, like an echo in the stillness. There was a ringing in my ears.

Sophia gripped my hands. Lips trembling, she struggled to form the words.

I twisted around to the ladies. "Tell me!"

"Poseidon's sacrifice—" one of them began.

"Tell me!"

Clymene stepped forward, my favorite among my mother's ladies. "The oracle has spoken. Oh, Princess Andromeda, I can't bear to tell you this.... You'll be chained to a rock at the sea's edge. For the sea monster . . . tomorrow morning." Tears streamed down her cheeks. She covered her face with her hands. "And on your wedding day!"

I don't remember how I got to the main hall. My father rushed forward to clasp me in his arms. "I won't let this happen," he said. But the nobles' faces were stony; an elder named Mylos was shaking his head.

Fineus hurried to my side. "I've sent my oracle to cast the bones once more," he told me breathlessly. "He'll slay another bull and observe the entrails." He touched my wrist, his movements quick and nervous. "My oracle will conduct the rituals a second time."

"Poseidon has spoken!" shouted the elder Mylos. "The god spoke to us through our own priests two days ago, the same message the Tyrian has given us even now!" He pointed a bony finger at me. "Poseidon wants the Princess Andromeda!"

"He cannot have her!" my father cried. "Has the god no pity? She's my only child."

"You are father to your people as well. A king must think of the greater good."

Another minister stepped forward. "We can no longer risk the god's vengeance," he said, and they all nodded.

"My oracle will repeat the rituals," Fineus said again, his voice unsteady.

I was so grateful, I reached for his hand. He looked at me and then down at his feet, but not before I'd seen the panic in his eyes.

We knew the results within the hour in the

women's quarters. The oracle's findings were the same. No one was surprised.

My father did not come to comfort me. Sophia said he was arguing with his ministers in the hall, still refusing to accept the decision. Mother wouldn't answer when I pounded on her door.

"She can't bear to face you," her maid Clymene told me. "Crying her eyes out, she is, and she'll take no food. Tried to poison herself, poor soul. Now she's vowed to starve to death in her room."

"She mustn't have tried very hard," said Sophia, spitting out the words. "I'll supply her with better poison—the slow-acting kind."

"Don't," I said. "You know what she's like. She never thinks about the consequences."

"She *wanted* to hurt you—she's jealous! She's always been jealous of you!"

"No, that's not true." I wanted to believe my mother's boast was a foolish blunder, that she had no wish to hurt me.

"Look at you!" Sophia cried. "Still defending her!"

"How could she have known the god would condemn me?"

Sophia's voice broke then. "Oh, Andromeda, I'm so scared."

I gathered her into my arms and stroked her hair as she wept great gulping sobs, like a child.

"How can you be so forgiving?" she whispered. "So brave."

I wasn't brave, just numb to the core of my bones. None of it seemed real. I expected some divine intervention. I kept thinking, They can't execute me for something my mother has done, something I warned her about. I even managed to sleep a few hours.

While I tossed in my bed, the monster crashed through the gates of our city. At dawn, streets were slippery with the blood of victims. News of Poseidon's demand had spread throughout the land; rumors of rebellion had reached the ministers. Now everyone in Joppa was demanding my death. As soon as I heard the news, I ran back to the men's hall.

"Of course you love your daughter," Mylos was telling my father. "But daughters and sons are dying in our streets. It's the king's duty to sacrifice for his people."

Somewhere in the debate that followed, my mother appeared, screaming hysterically. She grabbed my father's arm to pull him away from the ministers. "Poseidon's punishment should fall on me!" she wailed.

"The god *has* punished you," he said slowly. "You're condemned to live with this. For the rest of your life." He pulled away with revulsion on his face, and she stood blinking up at him. The hall was silent, all eyes on them.

"You're going to let this happen?" she said, pressing her fingers against her temples. When he didn't answer, she turned to me, her face wild with fear.

I stood watching as if the two were characters in a dream I couldn't escape.

"Take *me!* It was my boast!" she shouted over and over as her ladies led her away.

My father didn't participate in the rites that followed. With startled eyes, he watched a slave curl ringlets in my hair, a ritual beautification, just as they would paint the horns of a prize bull before its slaughter. The priests dressed me in a white sacrificial robe. I kept asking for Sophia, but no one seemed to hear my words.

"I'll wake up in a minute," I kept telling myself as they led me out of the palace. I was so unresisting, they threw aside the rope they were going to use to bind my wrists to the chariot.

Father followed the procession, leaning against a servant, moving like the old man he had become.

I remember Sophia running along beside the chariot, screaming curses at the guards until she lost her voice. I remember my heart throbbing at the back of my throat. I remember some small things with extraordinary clarity: a patch of rust on the bronze fittings of the chariot, a wart on the hand of the driver, an eagle soaring above the mountains, patterns of sunlight filtering through the round leaves of a fig tree.

My favorite wildflowers bloomed in the meadows, bright red poppies and blue anemones waving in the breeze. Peasants lined the road, trying to make their excited, curious faces solemn enough for the occasion. It was a glorious day, punishing in its beauty. How was it possible to leave this earth and never see another spring?

Though the journey was a short one, it seemed to take hours to reach the sea. I tried not to think of the monster's teeth tearing my flesh. But the thought kept intruding: Would I faint? How long would it take to lose consciousness—and what then?

I was light-headed from taking in short gasps of air. I made an effort to breathe normally. "I'm a princess. I carry the blood of my ancestors," I told myself. "I must die with dignity."

Still, courage failed me at the edge of the sea-cliff, and I threw myself at Fineus's feet. "Be my champion! Fight for me!"

I watched his lips part in slow motion. He gestured with open hands. "I tried," he said. "I had the oracle repeat the rituals."

Poor man. Even as I'd said the words, I knew how absurd it was, the idea of Fineus fighting a sea serpent. How Sophia and I would have laughed at this!

Sophia would have fought for me, with all the fury in her small frame. They had carried her back to the palace. It had taken four soldiers to subdue her. Just as well, I thought. She shouldn't have to watch.

I looked down the twisting path at the jagged

rocks and the sea beyond. Over my shoulder I could see the stricken face of my father as the priest stepped forward, holding the chains. I felt as if I'd received a sudden blow to the chest.

"Father, help me! Don't let me die!" I reached out once more to Fineus before they took hold of me. The dream had become a nightmare, and I was not going to wake up—not in this lifetime.

CHAPTER FOUR

*T*hey had to drag me down the narrow trail, my fingernails drawing blood on the guards' forearms. But when we reached the bottom and they anchored the chains, hopelessness overwhelmed me, and I stopped fighting. Their task completed, the men climbed back to the clifftop, where my father stood with the elders as if watching a spectacle or a temple dance.

I wanted to shout at him, "You're my father, you're supposed to protect me! *I'm afraid!*" But I could find no voice for my rage. Above my head, gulls pierced the air with their cries. Seconds passed with excruciating slowness. I forced myself to think calmly about the afterlife. Before they burned my body, Sophia would wash and dress me. My mother would place a coin under my tongue to pay the boatman for my passage across the river Styx to Hades, Land of the Dead. I prayed I would be treated kindly, allowed to roam the Elysian Fields, the pleasant but boring place assigned to ghosts who have offended none of the gods.

The sea was calm as a lake. I watched the tide creep up the sloping ledge, closer and closer to my bare feet, and prayed the gods would let me drown before the monster arrived. Still, it was difficult to believe in monsters with a sea as calm and sparkling as this. And hearing the thud of my heart, it was impossible to believe that my body would soon cease to function, would become a thing to be mourned and disposed of—if anything was left to dispose of. I suddenly felt cold to the core of my bones. What if there was nothing left of me to burn? Without a body, how could they perform the rituals necessary to allow my passage to Hades?

Panic rose in my throat. Was the monster even now swimming toward me? Was Poseidon watching? Would the god smile to see it tear my flesh?

"It's not my fault!" I shouted. I lurched forward, straining against the metal bands. They cut into my bleeding wrists but held tight. I fell to my knees. "It isn't fair," I sobbed over and over.

High above me a shadow, too large to be one of the gulls, floated across the cliff face. At first I thought it might be a vulture, but as I lifted my head and squinted into the sun, I saw the shadow was not a bird. Suspended above me was some sort of figure.

Was this the great Poseidon coming to take his own vengeance? I'd never seen a god, but I knew their bodies gave off a radiance that dazzles human eyes. This figure appeared to be human, a man. When he glided closer, I could see gold wings attached to his heels.

I felt a spark of hope. "Help me!" I cried. I struggled with my chains to rise to my feet.

Was I hallucinating? The figure circled once more, coming still closer, then dropped to the ledge. He carefully deposited a leather pouch before kneeling beside me.

A surge of relief took my breath away. Could this really be Perseus?

He pointed at the cliff top. "Those men chained you here?"

I nodded, speechless. I still couldn't believe he was real. "I'm to be sacrificed," I finally heard myself say, "to a sea monster."

If this was Perseus, flying through our skies with his winged slippers, he was younger than I had dreamed him. His face was beardless, his skin a glowing bronze against his blond hair, which was tied at the base of his neck.

"What have you done to deserve this?" he asked.

"I've done nothing. It was my mother, Queen Cassiopea. She boasted that we were more beautiful than all the daughters of Poseidon."

"Then why are *you* being punished?"

"Poseidon wanted me—or so the oracles declared."

"Your mother should be here in your place." He bent to inspect my wrists, frowning at the wounds I'd made trying to break loose, then turned his head to smile at me. "Yet there may be some happy destiny in all this. Perhaps we were fated to meet." Gently, he took my hands and helped me to my feet.

Here at last was the love story I had created in my dreams. I was living it. I wanted to reach out and touch the smoothness of his shoulder, but the chains held me back. Then I noticed the tide edging forward, almost touching my feet, and I remembered where I was.

My face must have registered my despair.

"Don't be afraid," he said. "I can protect you from Poseidon's sea serpent—with Athena's help." There was a sly sparkle in his eyes. "I've had some experience slaying monsters. Perhaps you've heard of me?"

"Everyone knows of your deeds, Perseus."

He brushed a strand of hair from my forehead. "Tell me your name."

"Andromeda."

"Andromeda," he said softly, then, rousing himself. "We're wasting time. I must free you at once. My sword will cut through these chains; there's no sharper blade on earth. Ah, your hands, they're like ice." But his eyes were on my lips, his breath soft against my mouth—

All at once a rumbling like an earthquake shook the cliff. Perseus had just enough time to draw his sword. There had been no warning, no tidal wave to announce its arrival. The seagulls had all disappeared.

The monstrous reptile was swimming straight toward us, head held high, like a great ship navigating in calm seas. Water washed over us when its bulk hit the ledge.

"Almighty Zeus!" I breathed.

We stood rooted to the rock as the stench of its breath engulfed us. Then Perseus jumped in front of me and raised his sword to slash the coiling snake neck. The monster's head reared back to lunge at the small figure. Holding his sword in both hands, Perseus used all his strength to bring down his blade. But it only clanged against an armor of scales. The egg-shaped head recoiled for another strike, its gaping mouth lined with teeth the size of daggers, its tongue the color of blood. Once again it darted forward, mouth open. The huge jaws snapped shut, but Perseus had feinted and ducked.

For an instant I saw myself mirrored in one red eye, the monster's roar filling my ears. Sheets of water drenched me as the great beast churned the sea, lunging from side to side, its dagger teeth snapping at Perseus. Again and again, the monster charged, its teeth clashing only to find that Perseus had jumped aside or used his magic sandals to fly out of reach. Then he'd double back, sword raised, seeking a soft spot between the scales. I prayed to all the gods he would find one.

Something cold slithered against my foot, and

the monster's tail coiled around my ankle. I twisted and clawed at the rock, my only objective to put distance between myself and the nightmare raging around me. I dug my nails into the moss, struggling to climb the slippery incline, while the horrible tail lashed against my legs.

The contest seemed to go on forever: the monster's bellows, the sword's clanging—flashes of sea serpent, flashes of Perseus. Then, suddenly, the roaring was cut off, replaced by a high-pitched scream. At first I didn't recognize my own voice.

"Andromeda, it's over." Perseus was panting. His tunic was soaked with blood. He gripped my shoulders, turning me around. "Look!"

A gray-green mass seemed to fill the shallow reef, staining the turquoise waters with blood. The head, severed from the neck, rested against the ledge, its terrible red eyes staring up at us. We clung to each other. For a moment I was conscious only of Perseus's chest heaving against mine and the taste of salt water from his cheeks—or was it my own tears?

"I was so afraid," I whispered.

"*I* thought the gods had deserted me."

I heard my father shout my name, and we

pulled apart, Perseus shaking his head at the bloodstains he'd left on my white robe.

The gulls were back, swooping down to feast on the huge carcass. Men were scrambling down the path. Soon my father was there on the ledge, saying my name in a voice reverent with relief, dropping the keys in his rush to unlock the chains. Everyone seemed to be talking at once. Only Perseus said nothing. He was examining the wounds on my wrists.

Father had of course recognized my rescuer. "Lord Perseus," he said. "You have turned aside a terrible destiny. I pray Poseidon will be appeased by your courage."

My champion smiled shyly.

"I am forever in your debt," my father said. "Ask anything, and it shall be yours."

"I think the gods, in their mysterious ways, have led me here to Andromeda." Perseus shot me a glance. His eyes held a question, and I nodded, smiling.

"I ask for your daughter in marriage," Perseus said.

"Wait!" a voice called out, and Fineus pushed himself forward. "She's betrothed to me! Today was to be our wedding day."

Perseus let go of my hand. "She's betrothed to *you?* Then why were you up there while she waited here alone?"

"Why give the god two lives when he's asked for only one?" Fineus pulled himself up to his full height, eyes level with Perseus's chin. "But now that she's alive, I insist on my rights!"

"You have no rights!" I cried. "If Perseus had not come along, I would not be alive for you to claim!"

"Enough of this!" Perseus said. "Can't you see she's shivering with cold—and exhausted?" He wrapped me in his cloak and helped me up the path to the chariots, leaving Fineus to follow in brooding silence.

CHAPTER FIVE

Sophia was radiant but still hoarse as she bathed me and bandaged my wrists. "You should rest," she managed to whisper. "Perseus will be with your father for hours."

"You think I could sit still? I have to sacrifice to Aphrodite, so that she will look kindly on our love." I smiled up at her. "I have to be ready when he comes for me. What should I wear?"

I changed my robe three times, settling on a plain white tunic with a gold belt. Then we gathered wildflowers and made garlands to offer to the goddess of love.

My mother found me in the women's hall, arranging irises and lilies on Aphrodite's altar.

"Can you forgive me?" she asked in a faltering

voice. Flanked by her ladies, she lingered in the archway as if afraid to enter the room. "I couldn't have gone on living if you had paid the price for my foolishness," she said.

I nodded slowly, realizing with surprise that I had already forgiven her. I was so happy, it was impossible to bear a grudge against anyone. Whatever poison she'd swallowed must have taken its toll. With shoulders drooping, lank hair, and dark circles under her eyes, she had aged a decade in the past week.

I went and took her in my arms. How frail she felt! I gave her a real hug, unlike the perfunctory kisses I'd always placed on her cool cheek. "Of course I forgive you," I said. "Look how it's turned out! I've dreamed of having a husband like Perseus. He says we were destined to meet!"

"I hope you're not going to be disappointed," she said. She could not meet my eyes. "The marriage contract has been signed, the dowry already paid—to Fineus. I can't think he would release you or your treasure."

"But he has to!"

"Royal daughters do not choose their husbands. You know that," she said with a smile that was meant to be reassuring. "Your father has already chosen a man of rank and property."

"Perseus is the son of Zeus Almighty. What better lineage than that?"

I heard her take a long, steadying breath. "Here is the way it must be. . . ." She stepped back, still holding my hands. "Your father has no wish to provoke a war with Tyre. And after your marriage to Fineus, our kingdom will more than double in size."

I freed my hands and stood, arms crossed in front of my body. "And you were sent to make sure I would give no trouble." I remembered how obediently I had gone to my death just hours before. "Don't you care about me at all?" I demanded.

Mother was looking at me with more tenderness than I had ever seen in her face. "Andromeda, hear me," she said. "If I could, I would gladly arrange things as you wish. But we will not prevail here." She hesitated, searching for words. "The truth is, we all must live in this world of men . . . and there is less pain in acceptance."

"Did you love my father?"

"Yes, after awhile. Just as you will learn to love Fineus."

"Never," I said. "I will die first."

We heard scuffling in the hallway, then the voice of Perseus, who had pushed past the ladies and entered the room with his long-legged stride. Two flustered guards came scurrying behind him.

"I want to talk to Andromeda," he said to my mother. "Alone."

Mother looked from me to him, frowning. But the tenderness was still in her eyes. "You shouldn't be here unchaperoned. Andromeda still belongs to Fineus—"

"The marriage contract has been cancelled—by cowardice!" he said. "Fineus should have been willing to die with her, if not for her!"

"It's not as simple as that. . . ." Mother said. "There are political considerations." She smiled then and shook her head. "All right, just for a moment." She waved away the guards. "Come, ladies, we'll wait in the garden."

With sidelong glances, they left us alone.

Perseus set down the leather pouch he'd had with him that morning and stood looking at me. "You're so beautiful," he finally said.

"Is that what you wanted to talk about?" In spite of my mother's warnings, I was conscious of being the happiest person on earth.

"Yes. I mean no. Curse it, I'm not very good at this." He shrugged and pushed back the hair from his forehead. He seemed ill at ease in the cluttered women's hall, with its silken cushions and overflowing bouquets. I had a sudden fear, sharp as a pain, that he had come to retract his marriage offer.

"I know you're grateful to me," he said. "But I cannot force you into marriage because I saved your life. Perhaps you'd prefer Fineus. He's a king, with great wealth and lands."

At first I could find no words to reassure him. I was so amazed that Perseus could think I might prefer Fineus. "I'm thought to be quiet and sensible," I said, smiling. "Perhaps I would bore you after the life you've lived."

We both laughed, nervous and uncertain.

"I wanted to be your wife long before I met you," I said. "Before the boast and the sea monster, before the engagement to Fineus, which was not my choice. My mother was here to remind me that royal daughters do not choose their husbands."

Relief shone in his eyes as he reached for my hands. "That's all I needed to know. Now I can go back and fight it out in the council."

"Must you go right away?" I took his palm and pressed it to my cheek. "I dreamed of what you would look like. I memorized the stories of how you killed Medusa."

"It wasn't really my doing," he said. "It wasn't even a fair fight. She couldn't see me. Inside my pack is the helmet that makes its wearer invisible. I had the winged sandals and Athena's bronze shield. I never had to look at her face."

"But, how could you see to kill her?"

"I backed up, looking at her reflection in the shield and reaching behind me—like this. Then I hacked at her neck with the sword. And here's the wonder! They tell of her hideous face, underneath all the snakes, but the face that I saw in the reflection was beautiful! Still, if I had slipped and glanced directly at her, even for a second, that face would have turned me to stone, just like all the others."

I pointed with my chin at the leather pack. "Is her head in there, too?"

"Yes ... I never let it out of my sight."

"Would it still turn flesh and blood to stone, even severed from the body?"

He nodded, his smile surprisingly shy.

"What a terrible responsibility. The gods must think highly of you. But tell me, my lord," I said slowly. "Since you had your pack with you, why didn't you just show Medusa's head to the sea monster?" When Perseus didn't answer, I said, more insistently, "Why didn't you turn it to stone instead of fighting it?"

He grinned sheepishly.

"You mean you could have spared us that terror—not to mention the risk?" I drew away, frowning.

"There was no risk, not if we were destined for each other! Don't be angry, it all happened so fast." He smiled down at the floor, then lifted his eyes. "I suppose I was showing off. I was afraid I wouldn't be impressive enough. I have no real wealth to offer you."

"Don't you know the whole world is talking about your victory?" I said then, shaking my head. "It was a magnificent battle, what I saw of it." I placed my arms around his neck. His cheek was soft as velvet, his eyes green, with gold flecks in the irises.

He traced the outline of my lips with his fingertips. I reached to touch his golden curls. Slowly, he bent his head to kiss me.

"Let go of her, she's mine!" a voice rang out.

It was Fineus, followed by my father and mother and the ministers, all of them crowding into the hall.

"Fineus refuses to negotiate," my father said. "He's threatening war on our northern borders."

Perseus released me and reached for his pack. "Andromeda, turn around and face the wall!"

"No, wait!" I cried.

I went to my fiancé and put my hand on his wrist. "Fineus, think of our future. Every day I would look at you and remember that you were too afraid to fight for me. And you would look at me and remember that, too."

Fineus shifted his eyes from me to Perseus, who was clutching the sack with both hands.

"Keep the dowry," I said. "Perseus will take me without it." I glanced at my champion, who confirmed this offer with a haughty nod. But my father would need to give his blessing as well. I turned to him next.

Mother was holding his arm, her face pleading. "We owe Andromeda this happiness," she said.

"Fineus, will that satisfy you?" my father asked.

Fineus and his two ministers consulted with their eyes, no doubt calculating the worth of the dowry, without the northern territories, without me as potential breeder of sons.

I took a deep breath and tried one last time. "Fineus, I haven't stopped growing, I'm going to be *taller* than you."

He darted a look at the pack Perseus was holding. I think underneath all the bravado, Fineus understood his choices better than he pretended.

"All right, Andromeda, as you wish. But you'll be sorry. You could have been Queen of Tyre!"

I went to stand next to my beloved. "I'll never be sorry," I whispered.

I saw my father nodding approval, my mother smiling at us, eyes shining with happy tears.

"We were scheduled to host a wedding this very afternoon," she said, with a hint of the old playfulness. "I suggest we resume preparations at once."

CHAPTER SIX

*F*ineus was wrong. I never for a moment was
sorry that I chose Perseus. After our wedding, which was joyful beyond my happiest dreams,
Perseus and I flew to his home island of Seriphos.
Along the way, we visited exotic lands, flying with
the winged sandals, just below the clouds.

Perseus's mother, Danae, welcomed me to my new
home, and Sophia, who traveled by sea, joined us within the year. My husband could have conquered the
world with the contents of his leather pack. But he
used Medusa's head only once shortly after our arrival,
on a tyrant named Polydectes, who'd been trying
to bully the lovely, soft-spoken Danae into marriage.
After that, Perseus knew enough to give back the gifts
of the gods—the great sword, the helmet of invisibility,

and the winged shoes, which had provided us with such a wonderful honeymoon. To Athena, he returned the bronze shield, which had helped him slay Medusa. He gave the severed head to the goddess as well, and she fixed its image on her shield.

Unlike so many others who were favored by the gods, my hero was content to be human. Both of us accepted our place in the natural order, and in exchange for this acceptance, the gods permitted us to live happily. We produced a dynasty of strong sons and sensible, beautiful daughters, and after we died, Athena turned us into constellations. But the gods never forgave my mother for her boast, and as a final punishment, they hung Queen Cassiopea upside down in the sky. You can still see her there today, looking like an elongated letter W. You can also see Poseidon's sea serpent, its coils encircling the North Star as it sparkles in the night sky.

FOR THE LOVE OF A GOD
Psyche's Story

CHAPTER ONE

Whether you believe the story of my marriage to a supernatural being, of living surrounded by powerful magic, is not important. What is important are the lessons it teaches, lessons I had to learn— that trust is necessary in order for love to survive, and that great love always demands an equal measure of sacrifice.

My name is Psyche. I grew up hearing that I was the most beautiful child ever born. Everywhere in the kingdom ruled by my father, people compared me with Aphrodite, goddess of love and beauty. When I grew older, people flocked to offer flowers and barley groats to me on the goddess's feast day. This worship made me afraid.

❤ ❤ ❤

Aphrodite is jealous of her beauty. She is fond of changing her mortal competition into frogs or lizards, or worse, making them fall in love with frogs or lizards when struck by her invisible love arrows. To appease her, I covered her altar with garlands of roses from my garden. But I could do nothing to stop the praise and offerings to me.

My father enjoyed all this. He liked people to think of him as father of a new goddess. I had always been his favorite, the only one of his daughters to resemble our beautiful mother, who died when I was very young.

By the time I was twelve, my two older sisters were married and living on nearby estates. Whenever we were together, I would catch their husbands gazing at me with looks that frightened and confused me. My eldest sister, Oriota, was tall and stern, with a long nose and dark, piercing eyes. Her husband, Theo, was small and slight, and a little afraid of her, I think. He, at least, behaved with dignity at family gatherings. But my sister Thessala's husband, a merchant named Pleuron, would sit staring at me hungrily while poor, square-jawed Thessala looked on. As often as he could, he would find some excuse to catch me alone.

I remember very clearly the first time this happened. It was a feast day sacred to the god Apollo. Pleuron grabbed me by the wrist as I hurried through the courtyard with a basket of flowers.

"Our little Psyche is turning into a beauty," he whispered in my ear.

"Please, Lord Pleuron, my sisters are waiting for me."

"Don't be in such a hurry. I just want a closer look." He loomed over me, his breath reeking of wine and onions. "You're like a ripe peach waiting to be plucked."

I twisted away, afraid of making a scene, afraid of humiliating my sister. But Pleuron was stronger than I was. "Just one taste of your lips, little peach—"

"Psyche, come here at once!"

The high-pitched voice belonged to Thessala. My cheeks burning, I followed Pleuron inside. How could I explain that I had done nothing to encourage him? My sisters had cared for me since my mother's death. I had no wish to cause them pain, especially Thessala, who would never in her life be called pretty. Yet in that same moment—and you will think badly of me— I was also intrigued by my power to make men behave like fools.

"I was just telling Psyche she'll soon be breaking

hearts all over the kingdom," Pleuron said with a wink in my direction. "Another Aphrodite, and still as sweet-tempered as a village maid."

I saw my sisters exchange glances. How they must have hated me! But they never let on. Instead, they dressed me in the finest robes and braided ribbons into my hair. "Isn't she beautiful?" people would murmur, and my sisters would nod their heads.

They must have taken satisfaction in the fact that as I grew into adolescence, there were no offers of marriage. We began to hear talk of a mysterious destiny the gods had marked for me, rumors of a prophecy that I was not to wed a mortal.

When I was sixteen, my father tried to arrange a marriage in a neighboring kingdom. In spite of my considerable dowry, nothing was concluded. My sisters were not surprised. "Poor little Psyche," Thessala said to Oriota, who motioned for her to lower her voice when she saw me standing in the doorway. One by one, all my friends married. A girl named Adrasta already had a sweet baby to hold in her lap. I stopped visiting her.

I used to study myself in the mirror, as if looking at a stranger. I could take no credit for the golden hair, the heart-shaped face, the dark lashes over blue-violet eyes. The gods, for whatever reasons, had awarded me this face. But what was the use of it if suitors considered me beyond their reach?

In time, I began to think of my rumored destiny as a kind of consolation, especially when I overheard my sisters talking about "the problem," a code word for my lack of suitors. Sometimes, even then, I knew they were gloating over it.

My father, whose eyes used to light up whenever I entered a room, began to find ways to avoid me. I took to spending more and more time in my garden, or dancing to some sad inner music in a lonely meadow.

We were supposed to marry young in the Greek lands. Marriage was the only way a woman could bring honor to her family. You either made a good marriage or you didn't; you either produced healthy sons or you didn't. Everything in our lives depended on this role. Yet favored as I was by nature, it seemed I would have no part in it.

My seventeenth birthday was a miserable affair. My brothers-in-law couldn't take their eyes off the bodice of my new violet robe. Every time I was unattended, Pleuron came and stood behind me, pressing his thigh against my hips while he offered disgusting flattery. My sisters gave me silver bracelets. My father increased my dowry by enough gold to provide my future husband with a chariot and matched horses. And still there were no offers.

At last my father decided to consult the oracle at Delphi. We had oracles in our own state, servants to local gods, but when matters were critical, people climbed Delphi's pine-clad mountain, bringing their problems to the priestess of Apollo, god of music and medicine. A judgment from Delphi was respected all over the civilized world.

Father was gone two weeks. When he returned, he had my sister Oriota with him. "My dearest Psyche," he began, then glanced at Oriota, sighing deeply.

"The prophecy is true," Oriota said. "Your husband is not to be a mortal man!"

For an instant I felt a thrill of excitement. At last, there was going to be a marriage—and to one of the immortals! But my sister's grim expression stopped me. "Who is this husband?" I asked.

Father reached for my hands. "We're to take you to the top of Mount Salulta on the morning following the next full moon. You'll be wearing bridal finery...."

Something in his voice was unnaturally brisk. "Will my husband be there to meet us?" I asked.

He shook his head sadly. "Nothing can be done to alter your fate. The gods have spoken."

"You're frightening me! Who *is* this husband?"

"We fear it's a monster you're destined for!" Oriota cried. "The oracles say he flies through the air. Even the gods are afraid of him." She pressed her hand against her heart; I couldn't help thinking she was enjoying the drama. "Whoever he is, he refuses to join the ceremony, won't even show himself."

"Then how can we be married?"

My father cut short my question. "I was not told how to conduct the marriage! Only to deliver you to the mountain. Psyche, do not ask us to refuse Apollo's summons. You know it would mean disaster for us all."

CHAPTER TWO

O riota stayed to supervise the wedding preparations, badgering servants and working herself to exhaustion as the dreaded day approached.

"We must put on a good showing, no matter what destiny the gods send our way," she reminded me often.

I did my best to follow orders, but I never seemed to satisfy her. I think she wanted me to be as horrified about my destiny as she was. But somehow I'd begun to feel part of a great mystery, and a sort of calm fell over me. I couldn't tell you where this serenity came from, but I was grateful for it.

"We don't really *know* my future husband is a monster," I said to my sister one morning. "The oracle called him 'Lord of the Hidden Valley.'"

Oriota, who was inspecting my wedding dress, looked up with an exasperated sigh. "Must you always live in a dream world? . . . Well, if it offers some comfort," she said, shaking her head. "Now stand straight while we pin up the train. You're the king's daughter. You must maintain your dignity. You must prepare yourself for whatever is to happen."

In truth, there was little for me to prepare. I was to bring none of my belongings to the mountain. My last day, I worked in the garden, putting the flower beds in order, saying good-bye to my roses. "I have come to prune you one last time," I told them, "and to thank you for all the beauty you have given me."

That night, as was our custom, I offered up my old dolls and toys on the altar of Artemis, the goddess who protects young girls and pregnant women. I prayed that she might look kindly on my marriage.

All the villagers were invited to the wedding procession the following morning. Father had spared no expense. My new robe, billowing behind me in a crisp wind, was of the finest semi-sheer linen, the color of eggshells. My sisters and their families walked along with me, their faces grim. The only joyful guests were Thessala's two youngest boys, who scampered ahead, mindless of the family tragedy. A full company of musicians led the way, their gay wedding tunes a strange counterpoint to the sobbing of the house servants.

Everyone admired my courage, yet it wasn't really courage. I simply wasn't as frightened as they expected me to be. I was actually relieved that I would not have to look at my father's solemn face, or listen to my sisters whispering about me any longer. Even in a wealthy family, an unmarried girl is a burden, because of the shame she brings. I was ready to remove that burden.

And as I walked along behind the flute players, I began to be curious about this husband to be. My sisters always laughed at how I managed to find something good in everyone. That habit was serving me well now. I was thinking, no matter how horrible he looks, perhaps he'll have a kind heart. Besides, I told myself, my sisters had both secured ordinary mortal husbands, and as far as I could tell, they found little happiness with them. It was their children who gave them joy.

The marriage ritual seemed to go on forever. The priests didn't know how to conduct a ceremony without a bridegroom. They argued over such things as who should take my hand and lead me away and what name to record for the groom on the marriage contract. They finally settled on "Lord of the Hidden Valley."

The leave-taking was worse. My father had been told to return to the palace as soon as the marriage was concluded. I was to remain alone. Wedding guests were supposed to toss nuts and candies at the departing bride and groom. But I was not departing. With bewildered glances, the villagers tossed them behind their backs as they started down the trail. My father embraced me silently, eyes brimming with tears. My sisters lingered to give tearful instructions about sending a message, hidden inside an ancient fig tree at the edge of the path.

"Our servant will check every day. We need to know *if* . . . ," Oriota said before turning away to be consoled by Thessala.

If I survived my wedding night, she meant. "I'll do my best to get word to you," I answered with some impatience.

Oriota gave me the oddest look, as if she was disappointed by my refusal to weep over my terrible destiny. They kept turning around and looking back as the procession snaked its way down the mountain. I stood waving until my arm ached.

When I finally lost sight of them, I sank down on a patch of grass, bone tired. I wondered if terror would descend on me, now that I no longer needed to maintain my dignity—now that I was alone on Mount Salulta, waiting for my husband to claim me.

The gods must have been watching over me, because I felt no fear, only an irresistible desire to sleep. I stretched out on my back, the afternoon sun gentle on my face. Above me, white clouds floated across a pale blue sky. I lay there imagining strange animals in their shifting shapes. My last conscious thought was of how surprised my sisters would be if they could see me taking a nap.

I dreamed a fantastic dream. I was airborne, flying across green peaks, drifting through clouds, skimming over sheep grazing on green hillsides and over apple orchards in neat grids, tiny trees studded with red fruit. It was as if I were being carried in the arms of an invisible god. Then I was being set down on firm ground, with lush grass under my palms. I heard a voice say, "Have no fear, Psyche, for you are truly loved."

I opened my eyes and knew I had not been dreaming. I *had* been transported to another place! It was real, the bright sunshine, the trill of a lark, the scent of wild jasmine. I sat up, blinking my eyes at the most beautiful garden I had ever seen. Roses of every shade perfumed the air. A fountain splashed into a pool, its drops diamond-bright in the sunshine. I remember thinking that this was the kind of garden the gods must enjoy on Mount Olympus.

At the edge of the lawn stood a white marble villa, its doors open to a curved veranda with blue morning glories climbing the balustrade. I didn't pause to wonder how I had come to be there. I got up and walked to the veranda, stopping to pick a red rose and fasten it in my hair. Every living thing seemed to be pouring out its beauty just for me, and I accepted it without question. I knew I was in the presence of powerful magic, but I was not afraid.

Inside, a marble floor mirrored the swish of my robe as I swirled around the room. Then I had to touch everything. There were silk curtains blowing in the breeze, silver vases overflowing with roses, lush carpets in pastel colors, depicting exotic birds nesting in sprawling olive trees. You cannot imagine how wonderful it was. If a monster had provided this house, I had to commend him on his taste. It was nothing like our drab, drafty palace back home.

As I stood drinking it all in, a voice called, asking, "Are you hungry, mistress?"

"Who are you?" Turning around, I saw no one.

"We are your servants, mistress," two female voices piped.

"Where are you?"

"Over here," came a third voice, followed by a peal of laughter.

I followed the voices to a room where shutters were thrown open to frame a meadow of red poppies with a cloud-topped mountain in the background. I watched, speechless, as invisible hands spread a banquet on a table inlaid with mother-of-pearl.

"Wine, mistress?" Honey-colored liquid poured from a floating pitcher into a golden cup.

"Why can't I see you? Where *is* this place?"

Each time I asked a question, a platter would float toward me, and a voice would invite me to partake.

"Fruit, mistress? Cherries and strawberries, sweeter than any you have ever tasted."

"Quail stuffed with mushrooms from the Hidden Valley?"

After awhile I stopped asking and accepted the phantom servants along with the splendid food. As I dined, invisible musicians played the sweetest music I had ever heard. I watched the colors on the mountain soften from gold to misty blue and a pink dusk settle over the meadow.

My invisible companions cleared the table with giggling and good humor, and some whispered comments about me as I twirled around the courtyard breathing in the flower fragrances.

"How gracefully she dances."

"How lovely she is . . ."

"Hair the color of sunbeams."

"Eyes like mountain violets."

A voice called me to the adjoining wing, where a bathtub cut into purple marble was waiting for me. I undressed and climbed into scented water. Unseen hands sponged my back, anointed me with fragrant oil, then wrapped me in a soft towel. They perfumed my hair and piled it on top of my head, securing it with diamond clips.

A robe floated toward me, the softest of blues. I slipped into it, smoothing its folds around my hips.

"Now you're ready for the master," a voice said as it drifted toward the door.

"Wait, don't go," I called. But there was no answer.

Standing at the mirror, I tried to see myself in the half-light. My eyes glowed above flushed cheeks; diamonds sparkled in a crown of curls. I had never felt so beautiful.

The next room was clearly the bridal chamber. I sat down in a window seat and looked out at fireflies twinkling in the dusk. Somehow I knew I was alone, that all the voices had gone away. And only then did I begin to feel afraid. It was almost dark. I could barely make out the large bed, draped with curtains, on the other side of the room. When would he arrive? Would he be kind to me? What would he—or it—look like? I wanted to run and hide, but anyone who could control such magic would have found me wherever I went.

I sat hugging my knees until it was completely dark, a black, moonless darkness. When at last I heard the door open, I jumped to my feet, ready to flee.

"You have nothing to fear, my dearest Psyche." It was a new voice, deep and male, full of music and laughter.

I sensed rather than saw a dark form step forward.

"Where are you?" I whispered.

"Here." A rush of warmth shot though me as his hand reached for mine.

"I can't see you. Why aren't there any lamps?"

"See me with your touch." He lifted my hand to his face. He was beardless, his skin soft as the finest cloth.

"Who are you?"

"It must be difficult to understand all this," he said softly. "Please, don't be afraid. I would never hurt you."

"My sister thinks you're a monster."

He laughed. "Do I feel like a monster?"

I found myself smiling in the darkness. "Why can't I see you, then?"

He bent to kiss my palm. "I promise to love you forever," he said. "But I can't give you the answer to that question."

I was reeling from the sensations his kiss had produced, not just in my palm but throughout my body.

"Can you trust me, Psyche?"

I couldn't have explained why, but somehow I knew I could trust him in spite of all the mysteries. I knew this not just in my mind but in my bones. I moved closer and collided softly with his chest.

"Touch me," he said. "I'm real."

I rested my hands on his shoulders. His smooth-skinned body was so much firmer than my own.

"It's all right, we're married." He laughed, a gentle laugh, and I felt myself relaxing against him.

His tunic was of the finest linen; a metal clasp at his shoulder felt cold to the touch in contrast with the warmth of his skin. Beneath the tunic, fine hair grew on his chest.

I felt his breath against my lips and suddenly thought of my sisters. What would they say if they could see me? "What am I to call you?" I asked, pulling away. Part of me yearned to be kissed, part of me still wanted to run and hide.

"Ah, yes, Lord of the Hidden Valley is much too formal. . . ." His fingers were tracing the shape of my lips.

Overcoming my shyness, I reached to do the same. His lips were full, his nose perfectly formed, his curls springy under my fingertips. I soon forgot about his name, about my sisters.

He put his arms around me, pulling me closer. "Trust me, Psyche, you can't see me, but I'm real, and I love you with all my heart."

"I love you, too, my lord," I whispered, astonished that I did, that easily.

This was no monster. I cannot explain how I knew. I can only tell you I knew beyond any doubt that my husband, whoever he was, was beautiful and good.

I lifted my face to be kissed.

CHAPTER THREE

I called him simply "Andras Mou," which means "my man," and for a while, I was happier than I ever dreamed possible. He came to me each night after dark and left before the first light. I would dream through the day, reliving each caress. I felt whole when I was with him, incomplete when he was gone. Still, the waiting through quiet, sun-shot days, the mounting joy as the sky darkened, these were all part of the magic.

Then one morning I remembered my promise to my sisters, and that mindless ecstasy was gone.

"Tell me what's bothering you, my love," my husband asked me that night.

"I promised to leave my sisters a message. In an old fig tree on top of Mount Salulta. They must be frantic with worry. I haven't thought of them. Or my poor father." I cuddled against him, drinking in the scent of his skin. "I feel guilty for causing them pain. I want them to know how happy I am."

"They thought you were marrying a monster, I'd forgotten," he said after awhile. "Of course you must write to them." But his voice sounded sad. How well I'd learned to listen, to know him through his voice and his touch.

He said, "I'll have Zephyr deliver your letter." Zephyr was the name of the West Wind, the same invisible servant who had transported me to this valley.

I wrote my letter the next morning. Three days later, my sisters' response appeared on my breakfast tray. They were overjoyed to learn I was alive. The family had been in mourning, having given up hope.

"Let us know when we can come meet your husband," the letter announced. "A servant will look inside the fig tree every day."

"Can they come see the villa?" I asked my husband as soon as he arrived that night. "That will quiet their fears."

He didn't answer. I could feel his reluctance, a solid presence in the darkness. "They cannot meet me, not ever. Nor will they ever understand."

"If I could just let them see where I live. It's all so beautiful, I want to share it with them." In truth, I wanted them to know I was no longer a failure. I wanted my sisters to be impressed.

He took a breath and let it out slowly. "All right, my love. I'll have them brought here by the West Wind, just as you were."

I spent the next days in frantic activity, issuing orders to invisible servants for the banquet I planned to lay before my sisters. Silver bowls and gold goblets were polished until they shone like jewels. The house was perfumed with bouquets of flowers, the lawn trimmed to the soft regularity of green velvet.

On my breakfast tray the morning of the visit lay a gold bracelet, carved with tiny roses. Beside it was a note from my husband. "To my sweet Psyche, who has given me gifts beyond compare."

My sisters arrived shortly before noon. Remembering my own arrival, I watched them drift down from the sky and land in the garden. Zephyr, the West Wind, remained invisible, which by now was no surprise to me. But when I reached Thessala and

Oriota, they were windblown and outraged at the method of transportation.

"I never saw anything like that before," sputtered Oriota. "We were there at the fig tree, our servants beside us, and suddenly, whoosh! Flying through the air! Thessala, pull down your skirt."

"Please, don't be cross," I said. "It's the only way of getting here."

Oriota fixed me with critical eyes. "This is all very odd, Psyche."

"We must look like survivors of a shipwreck," said Thessala, tugging at her robe.

I hugged them both. "You look wonderful! Come inside. I want to show you everything."

They stood a moment, looking up at the villa. I could see they were impressed.

I tried to explain about the servants, to prepare them for the daily miracles I'd become accustomed to. Still, they sat openmouthed as silver platters floated toward them and wine poured from suspended pitchers. In spite of their astonishment, they managed to enjoy the meal: trout with almonds, followed by lamb stuffed with dates and rice, peacock eggs, and delicate pastries.

While Thessala helped herself to more of the pastries, I could see Oriota testing the weight of her goblet to determine if it was solid gold. She would never have asked me, and I smiled at that. I should have recognized how jealous she was, but I was so happy to see them both, happy they approved of my home.

"Cherries aren't even in season and *these* cherries . . ." Thessala said as the fruit bowl floated toward her. "Where is this place?"

"And your husband?" interrupted Oriota. "Why isn't he here to welcome us? I've asked you twice, and you haven't answered."

I fidgeted with my napkin. For days I'd been trying to think of an answer to this question. "He's very busy," I said. "He asks you to excuse him."

"Don't tell me he's invisible, too?" said Thessala.

"No, not really." I felt my cheeks burning.

"Well, what?" Oriota set down her goblet.

"All the rest of them are invisible," Thessala said, giggling.

"Just what have you gotten yourself into here?" Oriota said to me, aiming a sharp look in Thessala's direction.

It was useless to remind her that I had done nothing to arrange this marriage. Oriota's real quarrel was that I was happy in it.

"My husband is a merchant," I said. "He has to travel."

Under Oriota's frowning scrutiny, I told a story about an older man who showered me with presents because he needed to be away so much of the time. It was a bad lie. They left earlier than I had planned, their faces disapproving. I spent the rest of the day torn between guilt and resentment.

My husband found me huddled in the window seat. He reached for me and nuzzled my neck, and I sank back into the circle of his arms.

"What did you tell them about me?" he asked.

"That you're a merchant who has to travel. I don't think they believed me."

"Psyche, are you unhappy here?"

"No, my lord." I picked up his hand and kissed it. "I'm happier than I've ever been in my life. But I couldn't make them understand what I don't understand myself." I was silent a moment. "Why can't I see you?"

"I can't answer that question. I can only ask you to trust me."

"I do trust you . . . but there are so many secrets." I felt my eyes fill with tears. "What will I tell them? They want to come back next week. I'm hoping they'll bring my father. Oriota insists on meeting you."

"She's not what she seems. She's jealous of you."

"How can you say that? They've been like mothers to me, both of them."

If I had listened to my husband, I would have been spared a great deal of pain. But my sisters were all I had. I did not want to think they wished me ill, though I now know that to be true. "I miss them," I said, choking back the tears, and that was true, too.

"And you're all alone here during the day. How selfish of me." He stroked a strand of hair from my forehead. "Of course, write your letter. I'll see it's delivered to them."

CHAPTER FOUR

*T*his time, my sisters began their interrogation before we went in to lunch: "What sort of merchant?" "Where exactly does he travel?" "Didn't the prophecy state that your husband would not be an ordinary mortal?"

I struggled to invent answers to these questions. After awhile the lies got so complicated, I couldn't keep them straight. I kept changing the subject; Oriota kept changing it back. By the time the main course, duckling in wild plum sauce, arrived, I was wishing I had never invited them.

"At least tell us what he looks like," Oriota said, glancing up from her plate.

She caught me off guard. I had been day-dreaming and I responded automatically with the truth. "He's beautiful, with perfect features and soft, springy curls," I said wistfully, gazing out the window at the mountain. I was imagining the smooth firmness of his shoulders under my hands, wishing it was night and he was here with me instead of my meddlesome sisters.

"You're lying!" said Thessala. "You told us he was old, bald as a melon."

"Did I?" I couldn't remember. I blushed at them across our abandoned meals.

"Psyche, we demand that you tell us the truth about this situation," Oriota said.

Thessala reached to pat my hand. "We know what's really happening."

"You need not pretend all is well," Oriota interrupted. "It's clear you have married a hideous monster. Your sister and I are here to help you escape."

"I don't want to escape!"

"Listen carefully," Oriota continued over my protest. "He may be affectionate now, but when he grows tired of you, he'll find some way to get rid of you."

"That's not true! You don't know him!"

Oriota fixed me with piercing eyes. "Psyche, it

is time for you to face the truth. We're not leaving this house until you do."

"The truth is that he's beautiful." The idea of the two of them staying on depressed me beyond words. I hesitated, looking down at my hands, then I said, "But I don't know what he looks like because I've never seen him."

They both leaned forward in their chairs. "So he *is* invisible," breathed Thessala.

"He's not invisible...." I put down the napkin I'd been twisting and smoothed it out with my fingers. "He comes to me at night. After dark. I can see the faint outline of his body, hear his voice."

They were eyeing each other over my head. "Where does he go during the day?" Oriota demanded.

"I don't know. I don't ask."

"I can imagine," Thessala said, lifting her eyebrows.

"I know what you're thinking, but you're wrong! He's beautiful, and good, and he loves me!"

I felt disloyal discussing him with them. I wanted him to belong to me alone. I didn't want anyone else on earth to know the smell of his hair, still damp from the bath, or the taste of his lips. Most secret of all, I would never tell my sisters of the delicate wings I had touched with wonder on our first night together.

"Are you one of the mountain spirits?" I had asked, stroking their silken curves.

"No, my sweet Psyche, and I can't tell you more than that." He was smiling. I could hear the smile in his voice.

"But if you aren't a mountain spirit ...?"

He silenced me with a kiss. Just thinking about that first night made me blush, a sign to my sisters that I wasn't telling the truth.

Oriota was shaking her head. "Psyche, you tell us you're hoping to have a *child* with this ... creature. Do you understand what you would be bringing into the world?"

"I understand that I love him! And I don't want to talk about him anymore!" I threw down my napkin and ran out of the room.

"Love, such nonsense!" Oriota was saying.

They followed me to the garden. An afternoon rainbow arched above the mountain, a good omen. I was determined to put an end to their prying. This was my home. I was mistress here. They couldn't force me to talk about my husband if I didn't want to. Nor could they force me to go back with them. I began to relax. My happiness was safe.

But I was wrong. Oriota was about to find a way to convince me to betray him.

CHAPTER FIVE

*T*hessala was content to admire the rainbow, but Oriota was not so easily distracted.

"All right, suppose he's beautiful, just as you say," she began.

"I told you, I won't talk about him anymore." We were sitting in the shade of an acacia tree, watching a peacock display his colors. I was weaving her a headband of flowers, trying to engage her in talk of the garden.

"Don't be defiant, Psyche, it's not like you at all. Besides, I'm agreeing with you. Suppose he's beautiful and good, just as you say?" She broke a rose from its stem and handed it to me. "Then where does he go during the day?"

"I don't know where he goes. He asked me to trust him, and I do."

My sisters exchanged looks again.

"Think about it," Oriota said, pointing at the villa. "If he's as handsome as you say, and he controls all this, what's to prevent him from having another wife during the day, another house and garden? More than one."

I dropped the garland into my lap.

"Men do that," Thessala said with a sigh. "When Pleuron isn't chasing after slave girls, he's wooing the neighbors."

Pleuron's countless infidelities were a source of amusement in the kingdom. I always felt sorry for poor Thessala with her large, square body and whining voice. Now the image came, like a terrible nightmare. My husband, acting like Pleuron! Making love to another woman!

"Think about it, it makes sense," Oriota was saying.

I couldn't speak. I found myself thinking, If this is true, I will have to kill myself, but not until I kill him—and her. I looked down and saw blood on my finger. I had scratched myself on one of the roses.

"It's not true," I whispered.

"You don't know for sure," Oriota was saying. "You really don't know what's going on here."

I got to my feet and walked away, Oriota followed. "Psyche, listen to me. Haven't I always taken
care of you? Like one of my own children?"

"Please, let's not talk about it anymore." I was
having trouble breathing, as if a sharp stone were
lodged in my heart.

"You're surrounded by mysteries. You can begin
to solve them, by finding out who's in your bed."
She nodded gravely. "Tonight."

"You're not allowed to see your own husband,"
Thessala called out. "How could he ask you to live
like that if he really loved you?"

Oriota gripped my shoulders and turned me to
face her. My body was limp; I did not resist. "There
must be a lamp or a candle somewhere in the
house," she said. "All you need do is hide it in your
bedroom before he comes to you."

"I can't do that!" I cried. But I was still conjur-
ing images of daytime wives.

"He'll never know. Just light the lamp and tip-
toe to the bed while he's sleeping. It will only take a
second."

"Send us word as soon as you find out," Thessala said, coming to join us, her eyes gleaming
with excitement.

I swallowed down tears and shook my head, waving the two of them away from me.

I don't remember what I did to get through the rest of the day. All I can tell you is that seeds of doubt had been sown, and they sprouted into ugly growths. Suddenly, I had to know who this husband really was. Thessala was right. If he loved me, he would not force me to live in such doubt.

He never suspected. He thought I was sad because the visit had been another disappointment. I lay for hours curled in the warm protection of his arms, listening to his breathing. I had left the shutters open. I watched the stars change as constellations marched across the sky. When I saw the great scorpion rise from behind the mountain, I knew I had almost run out of time.

Very slowly, I shifted out of his embrace. I allowed my hand to rest on his before I rose from the bed and went to the chest in the corner of the room. Hidden behind it was a rusted oil lamp I had discovered in a cupboard on one of my explorations of the villa.

Hands shaking, I lit the wick. He'll never know, I told myself.

The wick gave birth to a small flame that I covered

with my hand as I approached the bed. I looked down at my husband. There in a pool of light was the most beautiful face I had ever seen, a face more glorious than a mortal could hope to possess. I was looking at a god. And in that sudden revelation, I even knew which one.

He lay on his side, one arm thrown across the pillow. My breath quickened. I drank in the sight of thick lashes, auburn curls, skin that seemed to glow from an inner radiance. I smiled down at the wings folded against his back. Then guilt washed over me like a wave. What had I done? He had given me everything and had asked just one thing in return. And with a god's wisdom, so much greater than my own, he had reasons for asking. It was clearly some sort of test, and I had not been equal to it. I knew then all that I had lost. I was desperate to return to our precious darkness, and in that flash of panic, I must have shaken the lamp. A drop of oil fell onto my husband's shoulder.

He rolled over and opened his eyes. I can still picture the grief in them after the first instant of disbelief.

Chapter Six

Without a word, he sat up and reached for his tunic.

"Please forgive me. I beg you, my lord." I wanted to cry, but I knew it would drive him away if I raised my voice.

He stood and adjusted the tunic, clasping it with a gold pin in the shape of a heart.

"Please say something," I whispered. My face felt stiff, my mouth almost incapable of forming words.

He turned to me, eyes full of pain. "I knew your sisters would bring trouble to our home."

"You're right, they're jealous! They told me to hide the lamp and look at you. They said you were visiting other women during the day!"

"No one forced you to believe them. You could have chosen trust over distrust, love over fear." He turned and went to the window.

I ran after him, sobbing, grasping. "Please, please don't leave me."

Gently, he pried my hands from his neck. "My mother said I could never trust a mortal woman to respect our mysteries. She was right. But I was too madly in love to listen. A taste of my own medicine," he added, smiling ruefully. "Psyche, do you know who I am?"

I nodded, tears streaming down my face. I knew. His name was Eros. He was the son of Aphrodite, the goddess people had deserted in order to worship me. His mission was to see that love flourished in this world so full of pain and death. His tools were a quiver of arrows, a bow, and a vial of love potion. Whenever he dipped an arrow into the vial and sent it flying, his victims felt the sweet rapture of love spreading through their veins—and all of a sudden loved another person better than themselves.

"You are Eros," I said. "Your beauty . . . your wings." I reached to touch them. "Why did you choose me? You could have any woman in the world!"

"It doesn't matter now." Tears sparkled in his eyes even as the lines around his mouth hardened to anger. "I can't stay here wanting to take you in my arms!"

I watched him step onto the window ledge. He spread his wings, looked at me for the last time, then took flight.

"Don't leave me, I'll die!" I cried after him.

When he vanished into the pink dawn, I knew that my life was over, that I had murdered myself with my own hands. Seeking the release of death, I climbed to the ledge and threw myself out the window.

How foolish to expect the short fall to the garden to end my life. I was only bruised, my arms and legs scratched by the rosebushes that had cushioned my fall. I smeared the blood with my fingertips. All the time I had spent in the garden, I had only seen the roses, never the thorns that guarded their beauty.

Not once during those first days did I lose myself in sleep. There was never a moment of release. I tried to kill myself but couldn't even succeed at that. When I jumped into the river to drown, the river god floated me back to shore, murmuring that death was not my answer.

I ate poison berries, but three wood nymphs found me and fed me an antidote. One of them, a lovely creature with turquoise eyes and a voice like wind chimes, dressed my cuts and combed brambles out of my hair.

"The love you had for Eros is still alive inside you," she told me. "In memory of him, you must share that love with all the creatures you meet."

"Please, let me die."

"Hush, child, hush," my protector crooned, rocking me in her arms as she sang a lullaby.

I aroused pity wherever I went, all the while loathing myself. I couldn't bear to suffer one more minute, yet each minute followed the one before. At last I decided to leave the valley, to climb Mount Saluta and throw myself from the peak. When I reached the top, I stood looking down at the bright green world I was leaving. The afternoon was warm and still. For the last time, I allowed tears to run down my face, salty on my lips.

Why wasn't I allowed an ordinary destiny? I asked the gods. An ordinary mortal husband who could chase after slave girls without breaking my heart? A sweet baby to hold? I stood a moment, shaking my fist at the universe before stepping off the rock into space.

There was relief as well as terror in that rush of free fall. Then I felt myself caught by powerful arms and borne high across the valley. I was flying without wings, just as I had the day of my wedding.

"Stop!" I yelled to the rushing wind. "I have a right to die!"

I heard a rumble of laugher. "Let yourself scream, you'll feel better," said a breathy voice.

My rescuer was Zephyr, the West Wind. This time he set me down beside a gurgling stream in a patch of woods.

"Now, then," the voice began, "I have a story to tell you. I ask you to sit quietly and listen."

"Why can't I be allowed to die? Why can't I see you?"

"You'll have to trust me. There are good reasons for both."

"Trust." I sighed. "We mortals are not very good at that, as you probably know."

"Psyche, please sit down. I have much to tell you, and little time. Please." Whenever he spoke, the leaves in the clearing rustled in time with his words.

I sat on a flat rock, hugging my knees.

"When you were growing to your full beauty in your father's kingdom," he began, "peasants were deserting the goddess Aphrodite on feast days, offering sacrifices to you instead."

"I tried to stop them. I was afraid the goddess would punish me for their disrespect."

"I know that, so does Aphrodite. The gods, when they're not busy with their own affairs, are capable of knowing all things here on earth. Nevertheless, Aphrodite has a jealous nature. It did not matter that you discouraged their worship."

"That's not fair!"

"We are not here to debate the fairness of the immortals, but to attempt to set things right. I beg you to stop interrupting. Aphrodite dispatched her son Eros with specific instructions: He was to strike you with one of his love arrows and arrange for a most unsuitable mate to be nearby. Use your imagination. The village idiot, perhaps a donkey or pig. Perhaps your sister's husband, Pleuron."

"How horrible!"

The airy voice chuckled. "Yes, isn't it? Aphrodite loves that sort of thing. Eros argued with her, said it was too severe a punishment, that your beauty was a gift of the gods. But her reputation was at stake. At other times, it should be said, she's capable of compassion toward humans."

"But I didn't fall in love with the village idiot. Or with Pleuron, thank the gods."

"Things went wrong. Eros, who was wearing his cloak of invisibility, slipped into your room one afternoon while you were napping. He stood a moment, looking down at you as he pulled the arrow from his quiver. How lovely she is, he thought, lovelier than any girl I have ever seen, on Earth or Olympus! He was so troubled by these thoughts that he pricked his finger on the arrow, just as he was dipping it into the love potion. So instead of you falling in love with Pleuron, Eros fell in love with you."

"I never knew!"

"Yes, you were unaware of this . . . inappropriate attachment. Suitors visited your father, but none made an offer, which is no surprise. A powerful immortal was making sure no man would ever have you. At the same time, the poor boy was pleading with his mother to let him marry you. There was no peace on Olympus with the two of them feuding. Finally Eros refused to do his mother's bidding, refused to shoot his arrows. Think of it. No more marriages, no new generations to offer sacrifices, no happy diversion of meddling in your amusing lives whenever we're bored. Something had to be done."

"She gave in and let him marry me!"

The West Wind sighed, stirring the leaves. "The marriage was a compromise. Eros could have you on one condition. He would put you to a test devised by his mother."

"Deathless gods! He would ask me to trust him, even if I could never see him." I hid my face in my hands, all the pain flooding back.

"Aphrodite was not surprised by your lack of trust. She expected it all along. But poor Eros had faith in you. Now the young man is disconsolate, moaning and crying and throwing himself in the dirt."

"My poor love! Is there no one to comfort him?" I was suddenly ashamed. I had not once thought of his suffering, only of my own.

"He'll survive, he's a god. The point is, we're back to no more arrows, no more marriages. Everyone on

Olympus is heartily sick of it. Which is why I'm here. And we have almost run out of time. Quick, take this."

A basket floated toward me. I lifted the lid and found a comb, a towel, some cosmetics—fragrant oil, face powder, alkanet juice for my cheeks.

"Make good use of these things. You can bathe in the pond. You're about to meet your mother-in-law. And Aphrodite respects beauty above all things."

CHAPTER SEVEN

*T*he goddess Aphrodite appeared at the center of the clearing in a pillar of light. She took form gradually, starting with her painted toenails. Her dress was the color of the sea in the filtered light of clouds, her hair the color of the first rays of daybreak. When her face emerged from the nimbus, it had such radiance, I couldn't look at it. I had to accustom my eyes, like coming out of a cave into full sunshine. I cannot adequately describe to you her fluid curves, her immortal grace. There are no words in our human language to describe the glory of the gods.

I fell to my knees. "Aphrodite," I cried. "I have served in your temple, offered sacrifices—"

Her eyes blazed. "Stop groveling. Stand up and let me look at you."

I stayed perfectly still while she walked around me, frowning. "Extraordinary," she finally said. "No wonder the poor boy is so smitten."

"Do you bring news of my husband?"

"He's no longer your husband," she said. "You failed to live up to the terms of the marriage. Remember?"

"I should have trusted him! I'll do anything to make amends!" I held out my hands to her. "Help me, please!"

She stood, arms crossed, the sun gilding her crown of braids. Her face showed no pity, so I was surprised by her next words. "Very well," she said. "I'm prepared to intervene."

Relief flooded through me like an elixir.

"In order to quiet my son's grieving, which is beginning to grate on everyone's nerves, I'm ready to offer you a second chance. I have four tasks to set before you. If you complete all of them, every one, you'll have your husband back."

"Thank you, merciful goddess!"

She waved aside my thanks. "Don't be so quick to thank me. You haven't heard what the tasks are."

I should have known how little mercy she would have for me. She wasn't offering a second chance at all. She was setting me up to be humiliated. She led me through a meadow to a shed hidden by laurel trees. Inside, she pointed her majestic finger at a pile of grain that occupied most of the floor, rising to touch the ceiling.

"You see before you a mixture of five different grains—millet, oats, rye, barley, and wheat. Your task is to sort them into separate piles."

"That's impossible!"

"If you want your husband back, you'll find a way," she said, smiling. "You have until sundown." Then, with a flourish of blue-green silk, she was gone.

I heard the bolt on the door slide into its casing, and sank down on the floor. Picking up a handful of grains, I watched them sift through my fingers. I had no tears left. Two small windows let a thin gray light into the room. There wasn't a single object I could use to kill myself. I cursed Aphrodite for offering false hope, and I cursed myself for believing her.

"Don't despair, dear Psyche," came a faint, high-pitched voice. "We will help sort the grain."

I felt tingling on my forearm and looked down to see an ant that was waving its antennae as if trying to attract my attention.

"Down here," piped the voice. "Yes, it's me talking to you."

I lifted my arm to study the creature at close range.

"That's better, now you can hear me," the voice said. "An army of my brethren is on its way to attack this hill. Rye, millet, oats, wheat, barley, all will be sorted by the time she comes back."

"But how? Why would you help me?"

"Because this is something we do exceedingly well."

I smiled, shaking my head. I couldn't believe I was conversing with an ant, but after all the mysteries I'd known, this was no more miraculous than invisible servants or goddesses materializing out of pillars of light.

"Thank you, thank you!" I cried to the other ants that were even now invading the room from every corner and crevice. It didn't seem possible that they could do the job, but a glimmer of hope was better than none.

They swarmed over the hill until it was black with their bodies, and still the columns kept coming. Throughout the afternoon the mountain of grain shrank beneath them. Five smaller mounds grew and grew, as columns and regiments of ants dispatched each seed to its proper place.

I had never really looked at ants, never noticed their energy and discipline, their wonderful earnestness. I made up my mind that I would never again kill one of these admirable creatures.

The final column of ants left the scene moments before Aphrodite's arrival. Her face flushed with anger as she surveyed their work. She stood a moment, shaking her head at the five neat piles. There was not a stray kernel on the floor, not a sign of my tiny accomplices. The goddess turned to me, eyes narrowed. "I don't know what trickery you've managed, but it isn't going to save you again!"

She was wrong. The second task seemed as impossible as the first, but once again I received help from an unexpected source. I was assigned to collect a bundle of gold fleece from some fierce sun rams that were twice as large as any ram I'd ever seen. I sat for hours on a riverbank trying to summon the courage to approach them. When I'd almost given up hope, I heard a whisper in my ear. This time the voices belonged to reeds growing along the bank. They told me to wait until noontime when the rams left the pasture to sleep in the shade. I would be able to gather the fleece that had caught on the brambles where they had grazed all morning.

I followed instructions and presented the golden bundle to my mother-in-law precisely on schedule. Like the ants, the reeds would not tell me why they were helping. Only later did I understand all the forces at work in my drama, and that each one was a lesson in love.

The third trial required me to draw water from a bottomless pool guarded by a dragon. This time an eagle befriended me, flying down to fill my goblet while the dragon slept. When I gave the water to Aphrodite, she took it from my hands without speaking, eyes blazing with outrage.

I was beginning to feel optimistic. I returned to my husband's villa for the first time, knowing the goddess would find me when she was ready for the fourth task. The servants welcomed me joyfully and brought me the first meal I'd eaten in all my dismal wandering. Afterward, I lay down on our bed and, instead of weeping and worrying, fell into a dreamless sleep.

The first thing I saw the next morning was

Aphrodite, standing in front of my looking glass. I jumped out of bed and hurried to greet her.

"There you are," she said to my reflection in the glass. She stroked her radiant cheek. "I'm looking a bit peaked, don't you think? All this family feuding has affected my looks."

"Not at all," I said. "Everyone knows your beauty is eternal."

As usual, she ignored my comment. "I want you to drop down to the Underworld and ask Queen Persephone for some of her beauty cream. It's her own secret formula." She paused, watching for my reaction. "Bring it to me. That's your final task."

I could hear my heart beating in the silence. "It isn't possible for a mortal to descend to the Land of the Dead and then return," I said.

"Then you shall have to be the first."

"How will I find the entrance? No, wait! Don't disappear! Tell me how!"

"Follow the setting sun," came the echo of her voice.

In spite of my long sleep, I was tired, bone tired. This fourth task was not so terrible, I told myself. I had been seeking the release of death. And death inevitably leads to that final journey across the river Styx to a land of shadows ruled by King Hades and Queen Persephone. There was no hope of returning. All that remained was to succeed in dying, once and for all.

I walked out of the valley with the morning sun on my back. In time, I came to a high tower and climbed wearily to the roof. I didn't pause to look down at the world I was leaving. But just as I stepped forward to jump, an invisible force thrust me from the edge. I heard a familiar voice say, "Things are not as hopeless as they seem."

It was Zephyr, the West Wind, again offering advice. "Psyche, listen to me. There is a way to descend to the Underworld and return to life."

I covered my ears with my hands. "Please, no more. I can't bear to hope anymore."

"Take heed of my instructions, for if you fail in the smallest detail, you will never again see the light of day."

"I don't want to see the light of day."

"Nonsense. Here, take these, and listen carefully." A loaf of barley bread and two coins appeared beside me. "The coins are for Charon, the boatman," he said, "to pay for your passage across the river Styx, both going and returning."

A spark of hope stirred. I lifted my head. "And the bread?"

"There now, that's better," he said, breathing softly on my face. "Be brave, dear Psyche. You're almost at the end of your journey. The bread is drugged. When you are ready to leave Hades' kingdom, you must give it to Cerberus, the vicious dog that guards the gate. It will pacify him long enough for you to make your escape. Some say he has fifty heads. That is not true; he has only three. Remember to break the bread into three pieces and give some to each one."

He carried me to a grove of black poplars. Just beyond it I saw the opening of a dark chasm.

"Down there. That's your path," he said. "You'll soon come to the underground river that flows into the Land of the Dead. While you're there, speak to no one but Queen Persephone."

A trail of vapor drifted from the opening, smelling of death. My heart was thudding in my ears.

"One more thing. Accept no food or water, even if they are offered. And no matter how tired you are, you must never sit down."

I will not dwell on the horrors I witnessed in that grim world. There are only the colors of shadows; all sounds are muffled in thick gray mist, and always there is the stench of death. My worst memories are of the miserable souls who pleaded for help. The first was an old man floating in the river as Charon ferried me across. I thought he was a corpse, but when we came closer, he opened his eyes and raised a withered hand, begging me soundlessly to pull him into the boat. He reminded me of my grandfather. I forced myself to look away.

I have no wish to relive that dreadful journey. I will tell you only that I followed Zephyr's advice and eventually reached Hades and his queen on their ebony thrones. Persephone had a darker, more haunting beauty than Aphrodite's. She sat silently, hands folded in her lap, face empty of emotion. You have no doubt heard how she was kidnapped by Hades, condemned to remain with him during the fall and winter, only allowed to return to her mother in the outside world during the spring and summer months. I felt profoundly sorry for her as I stood waiting to be recognized.

When I told her my errand, she seemed to spring to life. She agreed at once to share her beauty cream. And somehow she seems to know about my troubles. Handing me a small wooden box, she said, "Take this to your mother-in-law. Perhaps it will win her over."

Persephone spoke cheerfully enough, but I will never forget the sadness in her eyes. I found myself thinking of how she must miss the colors of the earth. "You are so kind," I said. "I don't know how to thank you." I hesitated, then added, "I wish I could bring you an armful of red roses from my garden."

She smiled sadly. "You must stay awhile, take some refreshment."

"No, I can't." I shook my head, remembering Zephyr's warning. "I'm so sorry," I said, and turned away from her terrible loneliness.

On my way out I managed to feed drugged bread to all three heads of the huge black dog, amazed that I felt no fear. Then, with my second coin, I paid Charon, the boatman, and climbed into his rowboat for the silent passage back across the black river. This time there were no lost souls pleading for help. I held the carved box in my lap, clutching it with both hands. I should have been feeling the wildest joy now that my trials were over. Instead, I felt numb. When Charon deposited me on the opposite shore, I didn't even remember to thank him.

Somehow I found the strength to climb up out of the chasm by keeping my eyes on the patch of light at the end. I stood there, blinking at the sunshine, savoring the colors. Then I went to lie down next to a pond shaded by pines. I closed my eyes and listened to the murmur of insects and the songs of birds. I breathed in the fragrance of pine needles. When I opened my eyes, I saw everything around me with amazing clarity. Green hills glowed in the afternoon sun, and all the colors of earth seemed to pulsate with light. On a nearby rock I watched an ant carrying a leaf almost twice its size. I was filled with tenderness for this tiny creature. A breeze in the treetops called to mind Zephyr and of all the others who had befriended me. I felt a connection to all things on earth.

Still, it was difficult to believe that my ordeal was over, that Aphrodite would take her beauty cream and allow me to see my husband.

I peeked at my reflection in the surface of the pond and saw a stranger with wild, tangled locks and the pallor of death on her face. Immortal gods, what if he no longer found me beautiful? What if, after all this, he didn't want me back? I pictured Aphrodite's astonishing beauty. How could a mortal woman ever hope to match the radiance of the gods?

Then I thought about Persephone's beauty formula. I had gone to such pains to get it; surely she wouldn't mind if I took a small dab for myself.

You will think me very foolish at this point in my story. I think so myself as I relive this memory. But I was so desperate to regain my husband, I gave no thought to the consequences. I reached for the box. When I opened the lid, an explosion of energy burst forth, knocking it from my hands. Colors blazed inside my head, and I sank into the sleep of death.

CHAPTER EIGHT

*T*he next thing I knew was a feeling of perfect peace. I regained consciousness cradled in loving arms, my head resting against a familiar firmness, the sound of my husband's heartbeats in my ears.

"My lord, Eros! I thought I was dreaming!" But I was looking up at his beautiful face, and it wasn't a dream!

"Dearest Psyche," he said. "You have no need of beauty ointment. You'll always be perfect to me."

"I thought you wouldn't want me. Look at me." I reached to smooth my hair.

"I'll always want you." He took my hands and covered them with kisses. "Your trials are over. You've earned the right to live among us. Father

Zeus is waiting to confer immortality on you, so we can be together always!"

"How is that possible?" I whispered, drawing in my breath. Never had I dreamed of such a miracle.

"All things are possible on Mount Olympus." Eros picked up Persephone's box and closed the lid. "But for now, I'd better take charge of this. Until you've eaten the food of the gods, Persephone's magic is too powerful for you."

My joy turned to apprehension. I said, "I'm not worthy to live among the immortals."

"Of course you are. You were not afraid to risk everything for me. You had the courage to walk into Hades. Olympus is not nearly so fearsome. They're all going to love you."

"Not Aphrodite."

"My mother has graciously accepted defeat. She's agreed to dance at our wedding." Eros grinned. "Father Zeus has been on your side all along—he's the one who sent that eagle to fetch the water for you. He's been wanting me to settle down."

"He has?" It seemed so strange to be talking about family matters on Mount Olympus, as if the gods were ordinary humans.

"Yes, and we already have a job to do. You and I

will be in charge of the happiness of newly married couples. When the in-laws start making trouble, we'll send our friend, the West Wind, to blow in their ears."

"I wish he had done that for me," I said. "Oh, Eros, I should have trusted you!"

He kissed my forehead. "I was wrong, too. I went along with my mother's test, but I had my own motives, too. I didn't trust *you* to know who I was." He was quiet a moment, then he said, "I think I wanted you to love me as a man, not worship me as a god."

"Could you have passed the same test? If you had never been allowed to see me?"

Shaking his head, he placed a finger on my lips. For a while, we sat in silence, forgiving each other, forgiving ourselves. "I could not go a day without seeing you," he said. We kissed then, and kissed again.

"I can't imagine never growing old, living forever," I said after awhile. "Will we still live in our villa?"

"You're missing your roses," he said, smiling. "And yes, we can stay there most of the time. Olympus will be our second home. Come, my love, the gods are waiting to welcome you."

Author's Notes

In all three of these myths, the heroine marries a man who was not her father's choice, a man she loves. That's probably why these stories appealed to me as a young reader. But that's not the way it was in ancient Greece. Marriage was a kind of business arrangement negotiated by a girl's father. After a life of seclusion, a well-bred Greek girl was usually married off in her early teens to a much older man. She brought with her a dowry, and she herself became her husband's property. The historian Xenophon quotes one such husband describing his bride in a way that would appall readers today: "She was not yet fifteen when she came to me, and had spent her previous years under careful supervision so that she might see and hear and speak as little as possible."

We don't know much about the lives of the common people, but upper-class Greek wives had no time for romance. Their job was to run the household, supervising a large staff of servants and slaves. Greek husbands were free to work out in the gymnasium and stroll around the marketplace, discussing law and politics. They enjoyed a lively social life away from home, often in the company of women called hetaira. Known as servants to Aphrodite, these women were trained to entertain men with flute playing, dancing, and other wiles. The most famous hetaira was Aspasia, the woman behind the throne of

Pericles, Athens' greatest leader. He was almost thrown out of office because of the power she held over the city-state.

Other men took young boys as lovers; poets and philosophers wrote of the most noble form of love as that between two men. Wives were necessary, of course, to produce children, but the hero, Jason, quoted in an ancient tragedy, complains that, "There ought to be some better way for men to breed sons."

Still, we know from other plays that there were strong, bossy wives, like Oriota in my Psyche story. We also know of some genuine love stories between husbands and wives, stories like the ones in this book. In Homer's *Odyssey,* perhaps the best-known myth of all time, the hero Odysseus risked everything to get back to his wife, Penelope. The poet Homer tells us that when Odysseus finally arrived home after his ten-year ordeal, he clung to her like a shipwrecked sailor clings to land.

But even the cherished wives, like Penelope, would have had none of the freedom many of us take for granted today. We have few accounts of what they themselves thought about their lot. So in writing these stories, I had to speculate, to put myself inside my character's skin and imagine what she might have felt.

Of the three young women in this book, Psyche is most typical of the social system the myths were meant to maintain. She has no expectations of romance, or even happiness, from an arranged marriage. But she's conditioned to want one. She tells us that: "Marriage was the only thing a woman could look forward to, the only way she could bring honor to her family." Psyche is ready to marry a monster in order to remove the shame she brings to her family as an unmarried daughter.

Like Psyche, Andromeda grew up knowing a marriage would be arranged for her, for political reasons. That much she accepts. But when the time comes, she is dismayed by her father's choice of husband—the strutting Fineus. Andromeda's mother has no power to help her, but we know that Greek girls in similar predicaments appealed to the goddess Artemis for help. This goddess sometimes turned the reluctant bride into a tree or a flower escape the arranged marriage, just as Sophia reminds Andromeda in my retelling.

Atalanta, the most rebellious of the three heroines, sees marriage as a kind of death: "To be a prisoner inside my husband's house, never allowed to leave except on festival days...." Here she speaks the historical truth. Aristocratic wives were confined to a part of the house called the women's quarters. They saw no men except close relatives. Servants did the shopping; husbands went off alone to parties. One man, whose testimony has survived in ancient court records, bragged that his sister and niece were so well brought up that they were even embarrassed in the presence of a brother or uncle.

I had Milanion promise Atalanta that he would not

imprison her inside the women's quarters. He tells her, "Thracian women have freedom to come and go." I'd like to think this was true. After all, Thrace was north of Greece, near the Black Sea, where the Amazons, powerful women warriors, came from. I really put those words in Milanion's mouth because I wanted to give Atalanta a happy ending. As a young girl hooked on the myths, I loved her for standing up to her father and refusing to be married off.

At the same time, I didn't want her sending her opponents to death, as she does in the ancient stories. So in my retelling I made her at first ignorant of the conditions of the race. After that, she's at least tormented by all the killing, even though she continues to win. The other two stories in this book remain closer to the original sources. But there is more to all three than I've included in my retelling.

Atalanta: The Rest of the Story

Some of you may know of another myth in which Atalanta competes in a boar hunt with Greece's most macho warriors. She manages to wound the killer boar, and her host, a prince named Meleager, finishes it off. Meleager, who has fallen in love with the beautiful huntress, insists that the prize go to Atalanta. The other warriors object, and Meleager is killed. Scholars argue about whether this young woman is our Atalanta, the runner, or a different heroine who happened to have the same name.

In ancient sources, Atalanta does not have the happy honeymoon my retelling suggested. It turns out that Milanion, who prayed to Aphrodite for help, forgot to thank the goddess afterward. I suppose he was so ecstatic about his beautiful bride that it slipped his mind. Some sources report that he also made love to his wife in a sacred shrine. Milanion and Atalanta were changed into a pair of lions as punishment. But maybe that's not such a bad ending, after all. People who angered the gods were turned into worse things. And, as a lioness, Atalanta was allowed to run wild with her mate beside her.

Andromeda and Perseus: The Model Marriage

Perseus makes his appearance in this book just in time to save Andromeda from the sea monster. Before that he had a famous childhood. Perseus's grandfather, Acrisius, had been warned by an oracle that he would be killed by his own grandson, so he took pains to have no grandsons. He locked Danae, his only daughter, in a high tower with round-the-clock guards. But the god Zeus, who could travel through walls, appeared to Danae in a shower of gold, and she soon gave birth to a son named Perseus.

Acrisius was smart enough to know that only a supernatural

being could have gained entrance to his daughter's tower, so he didn't dare kill her baby. Instead, he locked mother and child inside a chest with airholes on top and dropped it into the ocean, hoping they would drown, and so, technically speaking, their deaths wouldn't be his doing.

Zeus floated the chest to an island and arranged for a kind fisherman to open it and take Danae and her baby home. The baby, Perseus, who was after all the son of Zeus, grew up to be a gifted athlete. Meanwhile, the king of the island was pressuring the beautiful Danae to become his wife. When she refused, the king got rid of her sturdy son by sending him off to kill Medusa.

We know how this plan backfired, so we can skip ahead to Perseus's meeting with Andromeda. Some ancient sources have him holding up Medusa's head and turning the sea serpent to stone. Others have him showing off his prowess in a battle to the death. This seemed more believable to me, but I also had Andromeda scold him for putting them at risk unnecessarily.

When Perseus arrived home with his bride, he used Medusa's head to kill the wicked king who was still trying to force his mother into marriage. After that he had the good sense to give the head to Athena. And, just as the oracles predicted, he accidentally killed his own grandfather. Perseus happened to be throwing the discus in regional games and hit one of the spectators, an old man named Acrisius, in the head.

As Andromeda tells us in her final chapter, she and Perseus ruled wisely, offended none of the gods, and were eventually placed in the sky as constellations.

Psyche and Eros: Love Tamed

Psyche did become immortal, just as I promised in the last story. She and Eros produced a beautiful daughter named Pleasure. As the myth evolved, Psyche, whose name means "soul" in Greek, came to symbolize the soul's journey to reach God, having proved itself through great suffering.

People in Ancient Greece really did fear Eros and his arrows. Even their gods feared his power to make us behave like fools, to become slaves to the loved one. The Greeks generally distrusted love, which is why so many of their myths have unhappy endings, and Aphrodite, the goddess of love, portrayed as dangerous and spiteful.

The Roman Touch

All three of these stories were first written down by Roman authors, who were more likely to award happy endings to lovers. The Romans, who adopted much of Greek mythology and religion, tended to be more optimistic about romance than the Greeks. They changed the names and personalities of

Eros and Aphrodite, calling him Cupid and her Venus. In Roman retellings, the two are more likely to be helping young lovers than creating mischief with their magic arrows.

Beyond the Stereotypes

I said earlier that we have few accounts written by women. The truth is that some women were writing. We know of at least sixteen prominent women poets in ancient Greece, but only fragments of their manuscripts have survived. A woman named Sappho was greatly respected, even by establishment males like the philosopher Plato. We have snippets of her poems because, by some lucky accident, they were used as packing for a mummified crocodile found in an Egyptian pyramid.

Sappho prayed to Aphrodite and wrote passionate love poems, some addressed to other women. Like many male contemporaries, she probably was bisexual, and the word "lesbian" comes from her home island of Lesbos. We can only wonder how she came to have such freedom.

Earlier poets like Homer wrote in the third person, from a respectable distance, about the deeds of heroes. Sappho wrote her poems in the first person. She gave us the world's first "I"—the individual self in all its joy and pain. One poem describes watching an ex-lover with her new love and being consumed by jealousy:

❤   ❤   ❤

And the sweat breaks running upon me, fever shakes my
body, paler I turn than grass is; I can feel that I have been
changed, I feel that death has come near me.

In this consuming passion, Sappho reminds us of the stories
in this book—and of the suffering of a young woman today, who
has just spotted her ex-boyfriend at the high-school dance with
his new girlfriend. Legend tells us Sappho ended her life by
jumping off a cliff in despair over a lover. Her desperate love
made her suicidal, just like Psyche in this book. No wonder the
Greeks feared love.

We would like to think that we live in a more enlightened
age, that we have come a long way from the ancient Greeks
with their love arrows and male dominance. True, a small
number of the world's women now have power to control
their own lives, at least financially. But we have only to turn
on the television to see the same love-struck madness that
made the Greeks fear the power of Aphrodite. Human
beings, both women and men, still do foolish and self-
destructive things in the name of love. The women in this
book are not so alien after all. And reaching down through
the centuries, their stories still speak to us of the dangerous
and wonderful power of romantic love—a power that delights
and terrorizes us to this day.